HOUSE OF SECRETS

Recent Titles by Helen Cannam from Severn House

A CLOUDED SKY
FAMILY BUSINESS
FIRST PARISH
THE HIGHWAYMAN
A PROUD LADY
QUEEN OF THE ROAD

HOUSE OF SECRETS

Helen Cannam

This title first published in Great Britain 2002 by
SEVERN HOUSE PUBLISHERS LTD of
9–15 High Street, Sutton, Surrey SM1 1DF.
Originally published 1984 in Great Britain by Robert Hale Ltd
under the title *September Harvest* and pseudonym *Mary Corrigan*.
This title first published in the USA 2002 by
SEVERN HOUSE PUBLISHERS INC., of
595 Madison Avenue, New York, NY 10022.

British Library Cataloguing in Publication Data

Cannam, Helen
     House of secrets
     1.   London (England) - History - 17th century - Fiction
     2.   Love stories
     I.   Title
     823.9'14 [F]

     ISBN 0-7278-5882-3

Printed and bound in Great Britain by
MPG Books Ltd, Bodmin, Cornwall.

Author's Note

I welcome the return to print of this early novel of mine, though the young mother who wrote it, scribbling away after the children were in bed, seems very far removed from the person – and writer – I am now.

First published under a pen-name in the early 1980's, it was, in a sense, an apprentice work. But it was great fun to do, and I shall never forget the delight of seeing my own words in print for the first time. I hope it is still able to give pleasure to those who read it.

ONE

When Olivia returned home later that morning with her shopping basket still light on her arm the house next door was marked with a red cross.

She stood quite still where she was in the middle of the empty street and stared at it. The stark red lines against the light smooth wood of the front door might have been marked in fire, so deeply did they burn into her brain. And yet she felt deadly cold, chilled and numb, shivering a little in the hot September sun.

She was dimly aware of someone approaching along the street, pausing close by; and then carefully, pointedly, crossing to the far side where the neat doors had no mark upon them. The steps died away, leaving her alone again.

She stood gazing at the door for what might have been minutes, or might have been only seconds. And then she drew a deep breath, pulled her cloak more closely about her, and turned towards her own front door.

Inside, she closed the door and paused in the dimness of the passage. How could she face them all, with this new knowledge upon her? The children must not know —

A small figure came clattering towards her down the stairs, fair curls bouncing, eyes bright.

"Aunt Livvy — Aunt Livvy — my tooth's come out!"

Olivia gazed absently at the tiny perfect white object clasped in Paulina's small hand, and forced a smile.

"Has it, my love? Then we must hide it under your pillow for the fairies to find." She put her arm about the child and drew her closer. "Where's Jane, Paulina?"

"Upstairs, Aunt Livvy."

Olivia set her basket down on the table in the passage and mounted the stairs, with the little girl clinging to her hand, chattering too eagerly to notice her aunt's inexplicable silence.

Jane, the only servant left at home, was in the children's room, soothing two year old William after one of his customary tantrums. The second child, five year old Barbara, stood looking on with reproachful gravity. In the doorway Olivia released Paulina's hand.

"Go and play with your doll, my poppet," she commanded. "Jane, I must speak with you —"

The servant looked up, anxiety sharp in her eyes as she caught Olivia's expression. She set William down and followed the other woman from the room. On the small landing outside, Olivia said quietly,

"Jane, Mr Benson's house is shut up with the plague."

Jane's hand flew to her cheek.

"God preserve us!" she whispered, her face white. She sank trembling down on the low window seat which looked over the small garden to the rear of the house. From here they could see the Bensons' garden too, innocent in the sunlight. "They sent a servant away sick last week," Jane went on.

"I didn't know that."

There was a long silence. The two women sat without looking at one another, deep in thought. All this year they had lived with the knowledge of the plague which ravaged the city about them. For months now the bells had tolled and tolled as the dead were carried out in the dark for burial. They knew how the overflowing graveyards were closed, and great pits dug for the disposal of the bodies. They knew of friends struck down, whole families dead or dying. They knew that this plague was — some said — far more deadly than any known before, and that each

6

week thousands more died in agony. But only now did the full horror of it reach out and touch them, for only today had any house in this quiet street been marked with the dreadful, dreaded sign.

After a while Olivia said:

"I can't wait any longer, Jane. I must take the children away."

Jane nodded.

"Maybe they wrote for you to come, but the letter was lost. Or no one would bring it for fear of the sickness."

Olivia said nothing, and Jane knew she did not believe it. It had after all been three months since the children's parents had left home. Time enough to send half a dozen letters begging Olivia to bring their little ones to safety.

"You can go home, of course," Olivia said after a moment. Home, for Jane, was at Greenwich, away from the worst of the plague. More than once Olivia had urged the servant to leave them, for her own safety, but always Jane had refused. Now she could have no reason to stay any longer.

"Will you not need my help on the journey?"

Olivia shook her head.

"I shall manage. And I think my brother would prefer it if only I went with them. That is one fewer to risk bringing the plague on them." She spoke a little drily, aware that her own presence too might be unwelcome — perhaps even that of the children. But she would not allow that possibility to deter her.

After another little pause, Jane said thoughtfully,

"I remember that preacher you took me to hear, saying that the plague was sent as a judgment on London for the sins of the court. But I can't help asking why it is that the courtiers are safe in the country and it is only the poor folk who suffer so."

"It is always the same," agreed Olivia bitterly. "See how it is the common sailors who are maimed and

7

wounded in these wars with the Dutch, never the great men who made the wars. Or almost never."

"War at sea and the plague on land — and we do not even have peace in the city itself while the sickness lasts — did you not hear of the plot to take the Tower, uncovered only days ago? These are terrible times, Mistress Olivia."

Olivia tried to shake off the numbing horror which had clung to her since that moment in the street.

"They are terrible," she agreed. "But there is work to be done for all that."

"Do you intend to travel by day?"

"It would be best, I think. We are less likely then to meet with the dead as they are carried out for burial. As far as they can, they still do that at night. It is just that there are too many now —"

Jane stood up.

"Did you find any food to buy this morning?"

"A little. It's in my basket downstairs. It is hard to find any shops open now."

"I'll put something together for your journey," Jane offered, and made her way downstairs.

Olivia went to her room. She would gather her own few belongings together before she told the children of the impending journey. They were playing quietly enough at the moment.

'These are terrible times'. The words echoed in her thoughts as she took spare stockings and chemise from the clothes press and folded them neatly. It had been a terrible year for everyone, as Jane had said. Yet for her it had been almost a relief that she was at last not alone in her pain. For her the terrible times had begun on the day five years ago when King Charles the Second rode in triumph through the May sunshine to reclaim his throne. Though even then, through all the dark days, there had been Luke to share her feelings, to bring her comfort. Until two years ago, when he also had gone, and left her with no one to whom she could turn.

It was always better not to remember. Briskly, Olivia banished the past from her mind — as she did perhaps ten times a day — and rolled her clothes into a bundle, and went to the children.

"We're going on a journey," she told them cheerfully, as if she were promising them a rare treat. "We're going to see mother and father again."

It took some time to pack their belongings, eliminating all but the most essential toys, the few items necessary for reasonable cleanliness: Olivia valued cleanliness more highly than most people she knew. She would have packed more quickly without the children at her side to suggest that this and that must not be left behind, but she had not the heart to deprive them of the pleasure of helping. They had few enough pleasures these days.

It was early in the afternoon before they set out at last. Olivia was careful to leave the house tidy and in order, its doors and windows securely locked and barred, the keys safe in the pocket of her gown. At the end of the street Jane parted from them, kissing the children and wishing them well on the journey. Both women knew only too well that they might never meet again.

When she had first come to London the noise and clamour of the city had been unbearable to Olivia after the quiet of her country home. But in the past months she had almost wished that bustle back again, in the unnatural silence of the plague-stricken streets. People no longer walked slowly, gazing at market stalls or into shop windows, or gathered to talk on street corners. Only those who had to go out did so, and they wasted no time about it. Shops and markets and theatres had closed down, trade was almost at a standstill, only the tolling bells and the occasional voice crying in delirium from a shut-up house breaking the daytime quiet. At night alone were the streets crowded, with furtive torchlit processions of mourners, the rattle of carts carrying the dead to the burial pits, the cry 'Bring out your dead!' echoing between the high crowded houses. Olivia had always hated London, for the squalor and misery which dwelt side by side with the uncaring licentiousness of the court. Now it had become a living nightmare in which fear and death stalked the streets and lurked in the stinking yards and narrow alleys. She had longed many times to leave its horrors behind her.

Yet now she tried not to think of where she was going. Henry and Celia were staying in Oxford, she knew — and not far, then, from Spensley Abbey — No, she must not think of that. She must remember only that she had to take her three small charges safely to their parents, away from the plague which had already claimed so many young lives. It was the one thing which mattered.

The children enjoyed the first part of the journey, unconcerned at deserted streets and unnerving sounds, or the sinister figures of the Searchers, the old women with their tall white warning wands who searched the bodies of the dead for the tell-tale signs of the plague. The little girls carried the two bundles of clothes between them, and the food. Olivia carried William, for he was too slow on foot to go as quickly as she knew they must.

Late in the afternoon they left the last of the houses behind them and reached the open fields, green and fresh and welcoming after the heat and stench of London. The children's brief excitement had soon subsided. Now they were growing tired and hungry and footsore. Olivia found a grassy bank and they sat down to eat. Soon, she knew, she must find somewhere for them to spend the night. And with little money in her purse an inn was out of the question.

Shortly after they had eaten they came on a prosperous looking farmhouse, and Olivia walked boldly up to the kitchen door to ask for shelter. The woman inside opened the door only just far enough to see out, and demanded sharply: "You from London?" Olivia nodded. "Then clear off, or I'll set the dogs on you!" The door slammed shut.

Olivia bit her lip, almost tempted to hammer on the door shouting until they let her in. But she knew it would be no use. And somewhere a dog began to bark loudly. She had the children to consider. She turned away, and lifted William into her arms.

"Off we go!" she said cheerfully.

"Aren't we stopping here, Aunt Livvy?" cried Paulina. "You said we'd stop soon."

"My feet hurt!" complained Barbara.

"I know, my poppet. So do mine. But it's not far now." What was 'not far' Olivia did not know. Would all the country people be so deeply suspicious, so dauntingly unfriendly?

She tried five more times to find shelter, and always it was the same. Even the weary faces of the children gazing out of the dusk at the firelit interiors of cottage or farmhouse had no effect on the frightened country folk. The plague was too terrible an enemy to be subdued by common kindness or hospitality.

In the end they slept in the fields, huddled against a hedge where the children stirred in alarm at the unfamiliar night noises, and only William slept soundly.

Dawn found them cramped and chilled and irritable. They ate some more of their fast-dwindling supply of food and set out again, doggedly and in silence.

"Will we ever get there?" sighed Paulina once, and Olivia, knowing how far they had still to go, left the

11

question unanswered.

Half-way through the morning it began to rain, a heavy drenching rain which turned the hard baked earth of the road to mud and soaked them quickly to the skin. Barbara began to cry, softly and miserably. Somehow, Olivia thought desperately, they must find shelter.

They came at last on a ruined barn at the roadside. Most of the roof had fallen in, but Olivia led the children beneath what little was left, and made them sit close together there. It would do for a little while, just until she could find a house that would take them in, or even allow them to shelter in an outhouse. She knew they could walk no further in this rain, exhausted as they were.

"You stay there, my loves. I shan't be long," she encouraged them. It troubled her that they were too tired even to protest as she walked away. She prayed that they would be safe until she found help, and that she would find it soon.

Outside, on the road, she paused at the sound of a vehicle coming quickly towards her from the direction of London. She scrambled onto the bank, well away from the mud it would throw up in passing. It was a coach, she saw soon, the fine coach of a great lord or lady, with a gilded coat of arms painted on the side and four horses to pull it. Whoever rode in such comfort would not spare a thought for the plight of the bedraggled girl by the roadside, and three weary children.

And then, to Olivia's utter astonishment, a voice called sharply from inside the coach and it drew to a halt just beside her. A man opened the door and leaned out.

"Can I be of assistance, wench? My coach is at your disposal if you wish."

Relief and thankfulness flooded Olivia's face with colour.

12

"Oh, sir, God bless you for it — I cannot find words —" She turned back to the ruined building. "Paulina! Barbara!" she called, running towards them. "Come — a kind gentleman will take us in his coach!" She gathered William into her arms, and the girls followed, new energy giving them speed. At the coach Olivia lifted them in one by one.

"Are these yours?" the man asked as the children clambered past him, wet and muddy and dishevelled. Olivia ignored the dismayed tone.

"No, but they are in my care," she answered quickly, without looking up. And then she scrambled after them and sank down on the seat at their side. The coach moved slowly forward again.

For a moment or two she sat with her head resting against the soft velvet behind her and closed her eyes, savouring the comfort of the upholstered seat to her weary body, full of relief that the children were warm and dry at last. Then Barbara sneezed, twice, and she looked round sharply.

But the child's thoughts were quite clearly very far from the misery of rain and weariness. All three children appeared to have forgotten already everything that they had been through. Three pairs of eyes gazed wide and full of wonder at the man who sat opposite them, as if he were some angelic visitant from another world. Olivia turned her head to see what had drawn that rapt interest.

And it was no wonder, she thought then, that they were struck dumb with awe. She herself had never before sat so close to so splendid a gentleman. She had always thought the fashions of the court faintly ridiculous, the wide short breeches, the brief doublet which revealed the full shirt beneath, the multitudinous knots of ribbon. But no one could have called this man ridiculous, however lavish the amber silk of his doublet and breeches and the nut-brown ribbon knots which trimmed it, however full

13

the sleeves of his shirt and however rich the lace which edged his collar.

A phrase heard once slipped into her thoughts: 'Golden lads and —' she could not bring the rest of it to mind at present. But it fitted this man so exactly, in all the arrogant assurance of his youth and wealth and splendid looks. Gravely, Olivia ran her eyes over the tall lean frame, discernible even through the concealing clothes, the broad shoulders, the graceful indolence of his present pose, which yet hinted at hidden energy.

He did not, she noted, wear the heavy curled wig favoured by most young men of fashion — perhaps because his own hair curled so profusely on its own account that no wig could have matched it. The shining honey-gold curls framed a face tanned golden-brown by the sun of this long hot summer, a face from which blue eyes surveyed her as intently as hers gazed at him. Feeling a little odd, almost dizzy, Olivia thought she had never seen eyes so deeply, so intensely, blue.

And then she realised, disconcertingly, that those eyes were not watching her with simple curiosity. They rested now on the slender lines of her small waist, emphasised by the clinging wetness of her dark green gown, on the rounded curve of her breast concealed beneath the demure white folds of the gorget, the cape-like collar which covered the low neckline. And then they moved up to the pale oval of her face, the wide long-lashed dark eyes, the smooth dark hair pushed into the neat coif beneath the severe high-crowned hat. Olivia began to feel uncomfortable, over-hot, almost as if she were sitting only half-dressed before him.

Slowly, with growing dismay, reading the message of those blue eyes, Olivia realised that kindness of heart had played no part at all in his offer of a place in his coach. No wonder he had been so dis-

14

mayed to see the children! He had thought her alone, defenceless, an easy prey for whatever he had in mind. And, she supposed, lowering her eyes before the naked desire of his gaze, he thought her attractive enough to merit his attention. To most women that might have been a flattering reflection, faced with so undeniably splendid a man. To Olivia it was only deeply alarming.

She glanced at the children. William had subsided against her with his thumb in his mouth. He was already almost asleep. Paulina and Barbara too looked drowsy and at ease, now their first wonder at being confronted with such splendour had faded a little. Olivia's first instinct just now had been to demand that he set them down again at once. But looking at the children she could not do it. She could only pray that the gentleman had sufficient decency not to force his attentions on the unwilling, particularly not before children. It was not consoling to reflect that nothing she had heard of the court and its ways could encourage her to hope for such restraint. And that this man had connections with the court she did not doubt.

Olivia pulled herself very upright, folded her hands neatly in her lap, and gazed down at them, every inch the demure and respectable gentlewoman. She hoped her alarming companion would very soon find her appearance daunting in its reserve, and lose all interest in it.

When he spoke again, she started, her heart quickening painfully, afraid of what he might say. But the words, spoken in a slow, deep voice, a little bored almost in tone, were innocent enough.

"You did not tell me where you were bound?"

"For Oxford, sir," she replied, without looking up. She was annoyed to feel her colour rise.

"Ah! Then our ways run together. How fortunate!"

"There is no need for you to take us so far, sir," returned Olivia coldly. "You may set us down as soon

15

as it is convenient." She did not quite know what she meant by that. She had, after all, decided that for the children's sake she must endure his company for a little longer. She did not look up when he replied, but she could hear a faint note of amusement in his voice.

"I shall be only too glad to be of service," he drawled. "Tell me, what is the purpose of your journey? It would seem a little hazardous for a woman so young as yourself to travel alone with three such small children."

"I am nineteen!" retorted Olivia, looking up and blushing furiously as his blue eyes, bright with irony, rested on her face.

"Exactly," he returned, to her indignation. After all, she judged him to be not a great deal older than she was. But she kept that reflection to herself, and said as coolly as she could,

"I am taking the children to my brother, Mr Henry Warriner. They are his children. He and his wife have been visiting friends at Oxford, for the christening of their son — the friends' son, that is."

"You come from London?"

"Yes." She waited for his expression to change, for him to order the coach to halt, and drive her and the children out again into the rain. But he did not do so. Instead he was silent for a little, his eyes running over her again in that way which brought the colour to her cheeks. To cover her discomfort Olivia cleared her throat and asked, "I should like to know who I must thank for this present kindness?" The question sounded stiff and awkward, but she hoped its tone held more coolness than she felt.

"Alston —" he said. "Benedict Alston." He inclined his head very slightly. "Your most humble servant." The mocking tone contradicted the words, as did the airy wave of one long-fingered bejewelled hand. His hands, Olivia noticed, though lavishly adorned with

16

rings, were strong and brown — fine hands, beneath their foppish decoration.

She gazed at him thoughtfully. The name stirred an echo somewhere in her memory, but she could not remember why. Very likely he had been talked of in her presence, with other well-known names. Celia was fond of gossip about the court and its doings, the more scandalous the better.

"And you?" he returned. "You are unwed, I take it? And live in your brother's household?"

"I am the poor relation," Olivia told him drily. "My brother is so good as to provide for me." She could not keep the bitter note from her voice, though she was a little ashamed at her own ingratitude. After all, Henry had been under no obligation to take her under his roof. And without his rather grudging hospitality she might well have starved.

The gentleman who called himself Benedict Alston was watching her now with a closer interest than before. Olivia sensed that something in what she had said had evoked that disquieting scrutiny, but she could not think what. It could hardly add to her attractions to be known to be penniless and totally dependent upon others.

"Do you find the position irksome?" her companion asked. Olivia coloured a little, from shame this time. "I ought not to," she admitted. "I owe my brother and sister-in-law a great deal — I have always been a considerable burden upon them, I think. He is not a wealthy man."

"What is his occupation?"

"He is a vintner, but not as yet a very prosperous one. He has hopes, of course, and ambitions. But the sickness this year has been a blow to them, as you can imagine."

"Do not more people drown their sorrows in wine in a time of plague?"

"Not if they're dead of it. Besides, it is the rich

17

who buy wine, and they leave town at the first hint of sickness."

"A troublesome time indeed." He smiled faintly. Clearly the anxieties of ordinary men like Henry Warriner were far removed from his experience, and did not remotely interest him. Olivia, who generally had little time for her brother's obsession with making his fortune, found herself angered now on his behalf. This arrogant courtier had rings on his fingers splendid enough to keep a poor family from want for ever. How dared he be openly so bored by the simple needs of lesser mortals!

When her companion spoke again Olivia realised that his thoughts had already moved on from her brother's problems, if they had ever really lingered there at all.

"You have a sweetheart, I suppose?" he asked. His tone was deliberately casual, but his eyes still retained that disconcerting intentness of expression. Olivia felt a quiver of anger at the impertinence of his questioning.

"You surely do not imagine someone in my position has anything to offer a man?" she demanded with asperity. Briefly, she thought of Luke, who had never cared how little she had to offer in a worldly sense, but had been her true friend — the nearest perhaps she had come to a sweetheart. Only he had gone now, and there had never been anyone else.

To her astonishment her companion reached across and took her hand in his. His face had a new softness of expression, a warmth which was yet not gentle or even kindly. With a graceful gesture he raised her hand to his lips, lightly kissing it, and then held it imprisoned between his own, caressing it lightly. Olivia felt hot with embarrassment, but resisted the impulse to snatch her hand away. Paulina was watching them with all the gravity of her eight years, and Olivia did not wish to alarm her by any hint that this man was anything other than a friend.

"You have your beauty, sweet maid," he said after a moment, his voice slow, warm, caressing as his touch on her hand.

"That is not the first thing men look for in a wife," Olivia returned coldly. "And often not even the last."

He glanced at her, smiling, but made no comment. Olivia did not find the smile particularly pleasant. She watched as he turned her hand palm upward, stroking the roughened finger-tips, the places where hard work had calloused the skin.

"This pretty hand was not made for rough toil," he said insinuatingly. This time Olivia did withdraw it, as gently as she could.

"The Lord made all our hands for toil," she rebuked him severely. "If we do not make use of them then we give way to idleness."

"And the Devil makes work for idle hands," he added, his eyes bright with mocking laughter.

"Yes," said Olivia, unrelenting. "Exactly."

"Yet what would life be without idleness?" he asked lightly. Olivia was relieved when Barbara's voice spared her the necessity of answering.

"Aunt Livvy, my head hurts!"

Olivia turned, full of concern. Barbara did indeed look pale, her eyes very large in her small white face. She had never been strong, and she had suffered a good deal during the past twenty four hours. Olivia reached out and stroked her hair.

"Never mind, my love. We'll soon be there now."

When she looked again at her companion he raised a questioning eyebrow.

"Livvy?"

"Olivia," she told him.

"A pretty name. Severely classical — Roman. Not the Rome of the Empire, of course — so like this present debauched age. The Rome of the Republic, austere and upright. It suits you."

19

Olivia lowered her eyes uncomfortably. Had he realised how close to the mark his light, teasing words had come, almost as if he knew she had been raised under the short-lived English Republic, and named after its chief creator, Oliver Cromwell? But he could not have known, of course. Now, he turned to glance out of the window, and said casually,

"The rain has ceased, I see." Even that simple phrase had a facetious note, as if he were mocking her by making such trivial conversation.

"Then you will be able to set us down to continue on our way on foot."

That, she was pleased to see, did startle him. His eyes widened and for an instant the bored indolence slipped from his expression, like a mask briefly laid aside. But only for an instant.

"Now, my dear Mistress Olivia, I cannot believe you wish to subject yourself and the little ones to such discomfort again! The road is thick with dirt — and there are some miles still to go. Trust yourselves to me a little longer. You will reach your destination all the sooner for it."

"Please, Aunt Livvy!" Paulina broke in. "We don't want to walk any more."

Olivia sighed. There was no denying that it would be better far for the children to continue their journey in comfort. Their clothes were drying well now, and they were relaxed against the upholstered crimson velvet of the seat. And poor Barbara looked wan and weary. Also, it was most unlikely that her companion would do anything very dreadful with the children there. She found his conversation intensely irritating, and the arrogant assurance of his manner infuriated her. But she could bear that if she had to, for the children's sake.

"Very well," she relented stiffly. "Thank you — we shall be glad to accept your hospitality for the rest of the way." And then she closed her eyes, to show him that any further attempts at conversation would be unwelcome.

She must have dozed a little at last, for she awoke with a start to hear him say, "Ah, here we are!" and the coach jerked to a halt.

Olivia rubbed her eyes and yawned, and then realised that the man had already jumped down and was holding the door open for her, bowing with mocking grace. She stepped past him, and lifted the children after her, and then stood looking about her.

The coach stood on a gravelled driveway before a low ancient mansion of mellow stone, beautiful, tranquil in the evening sun. Fine trees scattered the parkland which stretched in all directions, and deer grazed beneath them. Close to the house formal yet pretty gardens set the golden walls in a fitting frame. It was charming, restful, enchanting even, and the children, released into the warm air, lured by the soft grass, ran laughing to play upon it.

But Olivia simply stood very still, gazing fixedly at the house from a face drained of all colour, clenching her hands fiercely at her sides. And then she turned to the man who had brought her here, and who waited, smiling slightly, beside the coach, and cried out in a voice sharp with anguish, "Oh, sir, how could you do this to me! How could you play so cruel a game!"

He came nearer to her, the smile still on his lips.

"Never fear," he said soothingly, "I bring you here only to refresh yourself a little before continuing the journey. There are some miles yet to go."

It was almost as if she had not taken in what he said. Her dark eyes were wide, haunted, full of horror.

"But this is Spensley Abbey!"

"And my home — But you know it, I see?"

"Your home!" The abrupt dismay of her tone startled him, as did her alarming pallor. He had not expected her to be pleased at finding herself here against her will. But such overwhelming distress was puzzling.

"Yes," he reiterated. "My home, Mistress Warriner, and —"

"I am not Mistress Warriner!" she cried. "Henry is only my half-brother. My name is Paris — Olivia Paris."

For a moment he said nothing at all. She saw his eyes widen, and he too had paled a little.

"Paris!" he exclaimed softly at last. "Then you . . .?"

"My father was Edward Paris," she told him quietly.

"The regicide?"

She nodded, her tone as bleak as her eyes.

"He was a lifelong friend of Oliver Cromwell. And he signed the warrant for the execution of King Charles the First, and he was hanged drawn and quartered for it when the present King returned. But you know all that — everyone knows it, I suppose. And you must know too that he bought Spensley Abbey when it was confiscated from the Earl of Alston after the Civil War —" She glanced up at him. "I thought I had heard your name somewhere. You are the present Earl, I imagine." He nodded, and she bent her head and went on in a low tone. "I spent my childhood here, the happiest years I have ever known. And you see how I came to be called Olivia — as a compliment to my father's great friend — he came here often to see us —" She raised desolate eyes to his face. "Please, if you have any compassion, take us on to Oxford now!"

What he would have said then she never knew, for Paulina came running towards them over the gravel calling, "Aunt Livvy! Barbara's been sick!", and she had to force herself to walk calmly to where Barbara sat crying miserably on the grass, and take the child into her arms. She was alarmed at how burning hot the small forehead was, though Barbara was visibly shivering.

After a moment, she became aware that Lord

Alston stood at her side, gazing down at her.

"How is the little maid?" he asked, with what sounded almost like genuine concern.

Olivia looked up, her eyes anxious.

"She is feverish, I think, sir — my lord. I thought it was simply that she was tired, but I fear it's more than that —" Her voice tailed off into silence.

'More than that'. The words hung on the air between them. They looked at each other, and she knew his thoughts were the same as hers. She had come with the children from London, from a city stricken with the plague —

He had gone very white. For a moment they neither of them said anything at all, and then Lord Alston spoke quietly, his voice shaking a little.

"You'd better get her inside, and into bed."

He drew back as she raised Barbara in her arms and carried her towards the house.

TWO

In her distress Olivia did not even notice the rooms through which they passed. The Earl led the way to a far wing of the house, where he opened a door and stood back to let her enter, William and Paulina at her side. He did not follow her, but paused in the doorway as she laid Barbara on the elaborately curtained bed: it had an embroidered cover, but no bedclothes.

"I will see that all you need is left here outside the door," he explained. "You are not to leave the room — you are none of you to leave the room — for any reason whatsoever."

There was no trace now in face or voice of the indolent courtier in the coach. His expression was grim and withdrawn, and Olivia sensed that he was still horribly afraid. She did not blame him. There was no man or woman who could look the plague in the face and not be afraid — she was afraid herself. It was not just the thought of almost certain death, but of a death so horrible, so agonising — She pushed the thought from her mind, grateful only that Lord Alston had not immediately turned them away, as so many would have done, without hesitation. The plague made men cruel, she knew that to her cost.

"And what of you?" she asked gently.

"I? — I shall leave here as soon as I have seen to your needs. I had in any case planned to return to the court at Salisbury tomorrow. I have no intention of lingering near the sickness any longer than I have to."

"But you might carry the infection with you!"

24

Olivia exclaimed. "You cannot take the risk!"

"Indeed I can. So long as no one knows there is a risk. I can thank God at least that I did not touch you overmuch." He shivered a little.

'Yes,' thought Olivia, watching him severely, 'now you are regretting your lustful impulses on the road. Even the chance of a little dalliance is not worth all this.'

He bowed his head.

"Good day, Mistress Paris. I do not suppose we shall meet again." And then the door closed behind him.

A little later Olivia heard steps approaching along the passage, and then retreating again, as quickly as possible. Outside the door now lay blankets and sheets, a servant's low truckle bed, a ewer of water and a bowl, food — anything they might possibly need. With the children's help Olivia carried them into the room and closed the door again. And then she set to work to make up the beds and settle Barbara to sleep.

"Aunt Livvy," asked Paulina after a while, "why do we have to stay here? Why can't we go out?"

"Because Barbara is ill and we don't want anyone else to catch her illness, do we?" returned Olivia as cheerfully as she could.

"Has she got the plague?"

Olivia glanced round sharply. Paulina's small face was grave, but no more than that.

"I don't know, my love, I don't know. Let's just hope she'll get well soon, shall we?"

It was not until the children had eaten their supper and were tucked up at last in bed — Barbara on the low servant's bed, William and Paulina in the great bed she would have to share with them later — that Olivia had time to think of everything that had happened to her today.

It all seemed so very unreal. The ride in the coach,

the attentive courtier. And now to be here, at Spensley, in this place which had once been her whole world, the place she had loved more than any other, the place where she had once been truly happy, as she could never hope to be again — And to be here like this, shut up with the plague she had come all this way to escape. It was strange, frightening, yet shot through with a ghastly irony.

Barbara had fallen into a heavy restless slumber, and Olivia left her side and wandered to the window. The garden lay quiet and warm in the dusk, the scent of late roses reaching her even here. As far as she could see the neat hedges, the little statues, the orderly beds were exactly as they had always been. There, once, she had walked, a very small girl, with the great men who had visited her father, as they talked of affairs of state and turned now and then to smile at her, or tease her a little, affectionately. She had been a special favourite of the Lord Protector Cromwell. She had a vivid recollection of herself at about Paulina's age, seated on his knee, as he asked her about her lessons, and her dolls.

Most of all the gardens were bound up with memories of Luke Marchant, her playfellow, son of her father's neighbour and friend, who came often to run with her along those grassy paths, to share her games, to torment and cherish her at once. Later, when they grew older, they would walk together talking gravely like small adults of all they cared about most deeply. He was so very like her, slim and dark, about her own age, thinking as she did on almost every subject.

Luke alone had stayed with her when they had come to arrest her father — her mother, thank God, had not lived to see that day. And Luke alone had been able to bring her a little comfort during the grim months that followed. For he too had lost everything. His father had died in prison, long after Edward Paris had gone to the scaffold. Luke, too, had seen his home restored to its Royalist owners, had found himself penniless, despised, his very name loathed and detested. He had come with her to London as her father was brought to trial, and lodged near her half-brother's house, and they had spent many sad yet consoling hours together, two aliens out of tune with the times.

Only, he had found this new Restoration England too intolerant and loose-living for his taste, and set out to find a freer, cleaner way of life in America. If he had not been almost destitute he would have taken her with him, she knew that. As it was, he promised that one day, if he were able, he would send for her to join him there, or even come himself to bring her back. But that had been two years ago, and she had heard nothing from him since, and did not even know if he had reached his destination. She thought now that it was unlikely they would ever meet again.

And now the chance, wayward impulse of a corrupt courtier had brought her back to Spensley, face to face with her past, with the happiness which would never come again. She wondered fleetingly what memories she would carry with her this time when — if —she once more left behind her the honey-coloured walls of this house which had been her home. But it was better not to think of that. Barbara was sick, and she loved Barbara as she did all her brother's children, and her only thought must be to care for her as best she could.

As it grew fully dark the child stirred and woke. She seemed scarcely aware of anything but her need for Olivia's nearness. Now and then she slipped altogether into delirium, crying out or muttering incoherently under her breath. Olivia knelt at her side, bathing her hot forehead, murmuring soothing words which seemed to go unheard. But perhaps, she thought, Barbara found some kind of comfort in

27

them. She was thankful that the other two children were deeply and peacefully asleep.

Later the moon rose full and brilliant, its light flooding the room. Gradually Barbara subsided again into that unrestful slumber: she had a long way still to go before there could be any hope of improvement — or of . . . 'No, I must not think of it,' Olivia told herself. There were none of the tell-tale plague marks yet on the child's hot body, the spots and the painful swellings which would remove all possible doubt. But she had heard that they often did not show until near the end, or sometimes not at all.

Olivia bent her head briefly in prayer over the child's quiet form, and then undressed to her chemise and climbed into bed beside the other two children. William lay curled up like a small animal, round and immovable. Paulina was sprawled across the bed with arms flung wide, leaving very little space for a grown woman to stretch out beside her. Olivia lay on her side, stiff and uncomfortable, anxious not to disturb the sleeping child by claiming her fair share of the bed.

She did drift briefly into sleep at some time during the night, for she knew she had been asleep when something jolted her suddenly awake. The moon was still high, the room quiet, Barbara's breathing harsh and uneven, but untroubled by any waking discomfort. Perhaps she had cried out in her sleep, and the sound had wakened Olivia, alert to the child's need. She slid out of bed, just to make sure that all was well. And then stood very still with one hand on the bedpost.

The door facing her had been thrown wide, and framed in its opening, swaying slightly, stood a tall pale figure, lit by the moon. For a moment Olivia thought with a tremor of superstitious fear that this was some apparition come to haunt her, the figure of death himself perhaps, waiting, watching —

But death would not choose that shape, and he

was real enough, standing there in his stockinged feet, his doublet discarded, his shirt open at the neck, his fair hair dishevelled and silver in the moonlight.

He took a step forward into the room, and Olivia realised with horror that he was drunk — not much perhaps, but enough to unsteady his step.

"You'll wake the children!" she whispered sharply. Lord Alston stood still, half-smiling, watching her.

"Come here then!"

Olivia remained where she was, uncomfortably aware of her nakedness beneath the austere white linen of the chemise, of her hair flowing smooth and dark about her shoulders.

"I thought you were leaving," she retorted. It sounded like an accusation. She had disapproved of his recklessness, but now she wished very much that he had gone. Drunken men were horribly unpredictable.

"I didn't, did I?" Again he took a step nearer. "I sent the servants away, though — most of them." His speech was only slightly slurred, but that did not reassure Olivia. If he was a hardened drinker he could consume a great deal with little to show for it. And now he had told her she was all but alone with him. She put her hand to her throat, gathering the folds of her chemise to cover her breast, for his gaze rested unpleasantly on the creamy skin visible above the low rounded neckline.

"Please go," she begged. "You increase your danger by coming here."

He waved a nonchalant hand.

"What of it? If I die, I die — let's live while we can —" As he took another step towards her she held out her hands, palms outwards, in a warning gesture.

"Get out!" she hissed. "I don't want the children disturbed — you'll wake them!" Surely he didn't want the clamour of frightened children shattering the quiet of the night — and interrupting whatever he had in mind?

"Come to the door then!" Olivia shook her head fiercely; but as he began to move closer yet again, she relented.

"I'll come," she said. Above all the children must not be woken. But her heart beat wildly with alarm as she followed him.

In the doorway he propped himself on the door jamb and faced her with folded arms, smiling still. Olivia came to a halt at what she hoped was a safe distance.

"What do you want then?" she demanded severely in a low voice, though she sensed it was a foolish question. He gave a little laugh.

"What do you think I want?"

She felt her colour rise, and with it her anger.

"How can you speak so — how can you even think so! Tomorrow you may be dead. Is this the way to look death in the face?" He bent towards her, and she recoiled a little, still clutching the chemise to her throat. "You are drunk, my lord!"

"Yes," he agreed cheerfully, "so I am, very drunk. Let's laugh at grinning death, Olivia, and be happy while we may —" This time she did not move in time, and his hand closed about her shoulder, drawing her nearer. Olivia stiffened, trying to resist, but for all his intoxicated state he was too strong for her. His other hand found her waist, warm and firm through the thin chemise. "'License my roving hands and let them go . . .'" he murmured, his eyes half-closed. "I'll show you how busy my hands can be, little Olivia —"

Both hands now were on her waist, and he had pulled her to him. She had not realised how tall he was until now, when her head was bent against his chest, averted from that hungry gaze. She stood very still, upright, her hands gripped firmly together to preserve her modesty.

But she could not pretend to be oblivious to the

30

caressing touch at her waist. Deep within her something stirred and woke to life, flowing through her like liquid fire as one of his hands moved up her back, beneath her hair, about her throat, to her chin.

"Where's that pretty mouth, Olivia?" she heard him say softly; and then he had her head tilted back, and he was kissing her, ruthlessly, relentlessly, harshly, as she had never been kissed before. She had not dreamed there could be kisses like this.

For a moment longer she kept her hands clasped firmly to her breast, her body resistant to the dizzying sensations which his touch had woken in her. And then her hands relaxed their grasp, fell to her sides, and she felt herself melt against him, aware of every hard line of his lean body through the thin folds of shirt and chemise.

The kiss went on and on, his mouth searching, probing, demanding, her lips parted beneath his, her eyes closed. She yielded heedlessly to the delight of his caressing hands seeking the rounded fullness of her breast, the smooth line of her back, the curve of waist and hip. She was lost, abandoned, possessed by desire, by the hunger of her body to become one with his. Soon her limbs would lose all power to hold her — even now only the strength of his embrace kept her on her feet. Her arms reached up and held him, her fingers thrust into the soft thickness of his hair, drawing him ever closer to her.

And then Barbara cried out sharply in fear, and in an instant all trace of desire fled from Olivia. She drew back from him at once.

"Damn!" she heard him exclaim under his breath. But his hands moved to her arms, holding her only a moment longer and then fell to his sides, setting her free.

Quickly, trembling and breathless still, she hurried to the low bed and knelt by the child. Barbara was awake again, but lost in delirium, turning restlessly

31

from side to side. With a shaking hand Olivia reached for the bowl of water and dampened the cloth in it. As she bathed the hot face and hands the soothing action seemed to calm her a little, too, clearing her head, slowing her disordered heartbeat. She did not hear any sound from the door, but when she looked round at last the Earl had gone.

Olivia was thankful for the demands of the sick child, keeping her busy and occupied. And grateful, even more, that Barbara's cry had brought her to her senses, just in time. For she had no illusions as to what would have happened if the child had not wakened. She knew only too well that she had been lost to everything but the desire of the moment, that very soon she would have yielded her body without hesitation to this man she scarcely knew and had no reason even to like.

She felt sick now with disgust and shame — shame at her own weakness, disgust at his cynical using of her for his pleasure. She understood how in fear and horror at the sickness under his roof he might have set out to numb his senses with drink. She saw how, once drunk, he might then have hoped to find a deeper oblivion in her body. But to understand was not to find it possible to forgive. What kind of man was it who could be so lost to all decent human feeling as to take that path at such a time? Only a man, her reason told her, so corrupt, so dissolute, that he was beneath contempt. She was deeply ashamed of herself, but she hated the Earl of Alston even more.

Towards dawn Barbara relapsed again into the heavy stupor of before, and Olivia climbed back to bed. She felt exhausted, her limbs aching with weariness, but she could not sleep. Her brain was in a tumult, full of disordered troublesome thoughts and sensations. She could not think clearly, but neither could she rest.

It was a relief when William woke, and then

32

Paulina. She urged them to silence, dressed them, and sat them on the window seat to eat their breakfast in the early sunlight. The garden looked fresh and sparkling this morning, as full of innocent normality as the room. It was hard to believe that anything untoward had happened in the night. Olivia almost began to think she might have dreamed it. But not quite.

She was thankful after all that the children had brought more toys with them from London than she had intended. It meant that they had enough to occupy themselves this morning, without growing too bored. If Barbara was ill for very long it might be more difficult to keep them amused.

When the sick child stirred again Olivia went with beating heart to examine her hot body for the marks she feared so much to find. But there was nothing there — not yet. Olivia drew a deep breath with relief, though she knew it might very likely be only a brief respite.

Half-way through the morning, as she smoothed Barbara's pillow and tucked the blankets about her for perhaps the hundredth time, the door opened and Lord Alston came in.

He looked extraordinarily different from the smiling dishevelled visitant of the night. Now he was fully dressed, grave, unsmiling. If it had not been for the pallor of his face, which hinted at an aching head, Olivia might almost have thought it had been some other man who had come to her in the dark. But for all that she felt her colour rise fierily to her hairline.

After a moment, he said abruptly,

"I was drunk last night."

Olivia wondered if it were an apology: if so, she suspected it was the only one she was likely to receive.

"Yes," she returned disapprovingly. "You were." The unsteadiness of her voice, and the uncomfortable breathlessness which assailed her, rather destroyed the effect of her words. But he was not, she saw, in a frame of mind to be aware of such subtleties.

He came a little nearer.

"How's the child?" he asked, still in that brusque tone.

"Much the same," Olivia replied. "Perhaps a little worse — but there are no signs yet —" She looked up at him. "Tell me, why did you decide to stay?"

He shrugged.

"God knows. I thought better of it, I suppose. And if I take the sickness with me it does not help me, does it? — Have you all you need?"

"I should like some fresh water."

"I'll see that you have it. You realise you may leave this room after all? There's no one but myself and a groom and one old servant left here."

"I shall not leave Barbara," Olivia told him.

"No, but perhaps the children would like to run in the garden."

At that Olivia looked up with a smile.

"Thank you, my lord — I think they would like it very much."

For a moment he gazed at her in silence, frowning slightly. And then he made a faint inclination of the head and left the room.

Olivia made Paulina promise faithfully to look after William, and keep well away from the lily pond — she herself had fallen in it once — and sent them down to the garden. She heard them scampering happily along the passage away from the sickroom, leaving a heavy silence behind them. 'Please let Barbara get well!' Olivia prayed. 'And keep the other two from harm.' Her heart aching, she bent again over the sick child. Whatever this fever was, she feared it might be too much for frail little Barbara.

It was almost a relief when Lord Alston came with the water, breaking in on her dark thoughts and fears. He set the ewer down on the table without a word and then stood watching her for a while.

"I notice she calls for you, not for her mother," he commented at last.

"She has seen more of me of late," said Olivia carefully.

"It seems an unnatural mother who can leave her children in the midst of the plague while she goes jaunting to the country without them. Even if she did intend to have them sent after her."

It was a thought which had many times occurred to Olivia in the few years she had known Celia. But that this corrupt and worldly man should dare to criticise her frivolous sister-in-law was more than Olivia could stand.

"We all have our weaknesses," she retorted pointedly. "And their mother had her reasons."

"I do not doubt it." His tone now was cold, aloof as his expression. "Let me know if there is anything else you require." And he left her.

As the day drew to a close Olivia wondered apprehensively if the night would bring yet another disturbing interruption. But she need not have worried. The hours of darkness passed without the sound of steps approaching along the passage, and the door remained firmly closed.

And it was just as well, for Barbara had grown steadily worse as the day progressed, and through the night she raved and shouted and flung herself about the bed in a terrifying wild delirium. No amount of bathing of her hot skin, no amount of soothing caresses could calm her. Olivia was reduced to holding her firmly but gently in her arms, restraining her so that she should not hurt herself, but helpless against the power of the fever. Even Paulina was unable to sleep, gazing from the large bed in fear at the small demented creature who was no longer recognisable as the little sister she loved.

When morning came Barbara was exhausted, weak, scarcely conscious. The new quietness would have been a relief if it had not told Olivia how very much the sickness had sapped what little strength she had. Dread settled about her heart like a cold hand. Very soon, in the next few hours, she would know the worst.

It was towards evening that the Earl came to find her kneeling by the bed with her fingers on the thin wrist of the child, anxious eyes on the still white face. She had paid little attention when he had come in once before during the day, and now she did not look round. Lord Alston stood at the foot of the bed, gazing down at the two motionless figures, his face without expression.

And then the child's blue eyes fluttered briefly open, and closed again, and she gave a little sigh and moved her head very slightly. Olivia reached over and brushed her cheek, and laid a hand on her forehead. And when she looked up her eyes were brimming with tears.

"It's all over," she whispered. "I think she is going to be all right."

Then she buried her head on her arms and wept with relief and thankfulness.

THREE

So it was not the plague. When Olivia raised her head at last she saw her own realisation reflected in the Earl's blue eyes. The severe lines which had marked his face since their arrival at Spensley — except when drink relaxed them — had given way now to smiling relief. Olivia even felt a little tremor of anger that he should be visibly more relieved that the sickness was not what they had both feared, than that the child had survived. Though after all Barbara could mean nothing to him, Olivia reflected, trying to be fair.

"I'll bring wine and food and we can sup together, my little Mistress Olivia," he proposed with a jubilant grin. Olivia raised herself slowly to her feet. For all her relief she felt very tired, drained of strength. And repelled that the Earl should try to turn the occasion into a matter for frivolous celebration. The last thing she wanted now was his company.

"I have all I need, thank you, my lord," she said very stiffly. "The children and I wish only to sleep undisturbed." William, in fact, like Barbara herself, was already lost in slumber, though Paulina sat watching them from his side, her clear gaze travelling from her aunt's weary tranquil face to the Earl's bright-eyed countenance, and back again.

Lord Alston reached out and slid his hand caressingly beneath Olivia's chin. But it was the look in his eyes, languorous with desire, which brought the colour to her cheeks.

"Ah, Mistress Olivia, what an opportunity missed! I always think it a foolish error to waste the night in

37

sleep!"

Olivia jerked her head free and bent to straighten Barbara's cover — unnecessarily, but it helped to conceal her face.

"The Lord made the night for sleep!" she retorted. "And, besides, this child may be past the crisis, but she will need constant care for a long time yet."

"You have a pious platitude for every occasion, I see," said the Earl disparagingly, as he turned away. "I'll leave you to your godly reflections, and do my drinking alone —"

"Then perhaps you would be so good as to let me have a key to this door," Olivia requested. The Earl glanced over his shoulder.

"Never fear, Mistress Paris," he sneered. "I like my bedfellows to have more of womanly sweetness than you'll ever know. You're too cold by far for my taste."

And with that he left the room.

Paulina's small forehead was faintly wrinkled as Olivia came, face flushed with annoyance, to settle her for the night.

"Aunt Livvy," she said. "Do you think he likes us? Sometimes I think he does and sometimes I think he doesn't. He sounded cross just now, didn't he?"

Olivia smiled at the little girl.

"It doesn't really matter whether he likes us or not, my poppet. He has been kind enough to give us shelter under his roof, and we must be courteous to him in return. But that is all. Now go to sleep."

All four occupants of the room slept well that night, soundly and without stirring while darkness lasted.

But downstairs in the vast moonlit hall with its carved screen and wide empty hearth the Earl sat alone at one end of the long oak table and scowled into his cup as he steadily filled and emptied it and filled it again. And then at last he swept the cup clattering to the floor and went out into the night and walked through garden and park until the dawn.

After breakfast next day Paulina and William went out to play, and when they returned, rosy and hungry, for their dinner they reported that the servants had come back to Spensley. Even without their information Olivia would have known it, from the increased sounds which reached her from within the house, and from the fact that a pleasant and kindly female servant now came to see to their needs. She was touched by the unexpected thoughtfulness which sent nourishing broths and tempting delicacies for the sick child, as well as an abundance of good food for themselves. She was also very thankful that the return of his servants meant that they need see no more of the Earl. Very likely he was as glad of that as she was. By the middle of the next day when even the children playing in the garden had seen no sign of him, Olivia concluded that he must have continued his interrupted journey to the court, moved to Wiltshire while the plague raged in London.

Barbara recovered slowly but steadily. But it was clear to Olivia that it would be several days still before she would be fit to travel. And she did not like to ask if the Earl had given any instructions as to how they were to reach Oxford. If they had to go on foot then it would be weeks and not days before Barbara could attempt the journey.

Now that the worst of her anxiety was over Olivia began to feel restless at being cooped up in constant attendance on the child's sick-bed. Outside, the golden sun of late summer flooded the garden, and the air reaching her through the window, when she opened it a fraction — Barbara must not suffer a draught — was sweet and alluring. It would perhaps pain her a little to wander among her memories in the garden, but she longed for fresh air and exercise.

After dinner on the second day Barbara settled peacefully to sleep, and Olivia looked round from clearing away the remains of their meal to see Paulina seated on a stool by her sister's low bed.

"I'll watch her now, Aunt Livvy," said the child helpfully. "You take William into the garden this time. I'll come and find you if she wants anything."

Olivia gazed at Paulina for a moment. After all, she thought, why not? She need not be gone for long, and Paulina was a sensible child. She bent and kissed the little girl.

"Thank you, my love. That's most thoughtful of you."

There was a short stairway which led directly from this wing of the house into the garden: Olivia remembered it well.

Out in the sunshine every step she took reinforced Olivia's impression that nothing had changed out here since she had last wandered along these paths over five years ago. She herself was older, a little taller, but everything else was exactly the same.

When she turned a corner into the fragrant sheltered herb garden it was as if she had stepped straight back into that lost childhood she had left here at Spensley. There, busily weeding beneath the low lavender hedge, was an old man at whose side she had pulled many a weed and learnt how to care for many a plant. He turned to look at her as she came towards him, and then he removed his hat and got stiffly to his feet, smiling broadly.

"Mistress Olivia!" he cried, and held out his hands with transparent delight. Olivia took them in hers, tears rising to her eyes, though she returned his smile warmly.

"Tom Nelson! — So you're still here after all this time? This is a surprise!"

He nodded happily, though his eyes too seemed more than usually moist.

"They said you were here, Mistress Olivia, and I did so hope I'd see you again — and here you are! But how's the little lass? They said she was on the mend — and this little one, now — is he one of yours?"

Olivia laughed.

"No — the children are my brother Henry's — you may remember him, perhaps. But he did not come much to Spensley. If you recall he was my half-brother by my mother's first marriage. Now, tell me, Tom, how are you?"

"I'm very well, Mistress Olivia, and Nan too — do you remember her? She'll be glad I've seen you." He shook his head, a little sadly. "Times have changed since then. I'm the only one here now who knew your father, you know. A good man, Mistress Olivia, and a kindly master. He did not deserve such an end, though I'd not say that out loud to any but you, of course. They said he died bravely."

"Yes," Olivia whispered, "so they told me too."

Tom patted her hand gently.

"He'll have his reward, my mistress. Never fear." After a moment of silent sympathy, he smiled again and went on: "Not that I've anything to say against the present master, now. He's young, of course, and a bit wild, like all his kind — but good-hearted enough, and not lacking in sense when he cares to use it. And not over-much like his father, I'm glad to say."

"Do you remember as far back as that?" Olivia asked with astonishment. Tom nodded proudly.

"Aye, Mistress Olivia, indeed I do. I was here 'way back before the war. Thirty years I've cared for these gardens. Now he was a bad 'un, the old Earl — no loss when he was killed at Naseby fight. A hard master, a cruel husband to his poor wife, and never sober. That's one thing you can say of his young lordship — he's not a drunkard like his father, whatever else he may be. He has his vices, of course — brings his wild court friends here, and their loose women — and that does the garden no good, as you can imagine. But for all that he's never been seen in his cups, to my knowledge. Nothing ruins a man more than drink, I always say."

Just as well, thought Olivia, that Tom had not seen his master the other night: it brought the colour to her cheeks even now to think of it. Perhaps Lord Alston was after all beginning to follow in his father's footsteps.

"You live in London now, they say," the old man went on. And then he broke off, and Olivia saw his eyes move to some point behind her, and he raised a hand deferentially to his hair. Olivia turned, and lowered her eyes as the Earl came towards them, and clasped William's hand tightly in her own. She wished she had seen him coming in time to retreat to the house.

"Good afternoon, Tom," she heard him say pleasantly. "And you, Mistress Paris."

"I'll be getting on with my work, my lord," said the old man, gathering up his hat and his basket of weeds and moving further away. Olivia wanted to beg him to stay near her, but instead she stood very stiffly, mouth firmly closed, avoiding the Earl's gaze.

"You were talking of old times, I suppose," he observed casually.

"And now I am going back to Barbara."

"Oh, must you indeed — so soon? A pity — but let me offer you my arm." Olivia felt a strong urge to refuse him angrily; but she had told Paulina that they owed him courtesy at least, and it was true. And William was watching her closely. The children made life very difficult, she reflected. She would probably not be here at all if it had not been for them.

Unsmiling, without a word, she laid her hand very lightly on the Earl's arm, averting her eyes from his complacent smile. They set off slowly along the path, away from Tom, with William running ahead of them.

42

"I thought you would have gone to court by now," she said after a while.

"Poor Mistress Olivia! — Disappointed again. As you see, I am still here. I understand that the court is in the process of moving to Oxford. It seemed only sensible to wait for it to arrive."

Olivia stood still.

"Oxford! The court is coming there?"

"Yes. Why not? Oxford entertained the court throughout the Civil War. The city has a long and honourable tradition of hospitality to its King."

"But I am going to Oxford."

"Then the court will have one more star in its firmament," he said teasingly. She found his ironic little smile unbearably irritating.

"I do not wish to have anything to do with the court," she asserted. "I think I shall return to London." It was his turn now to be astonished.

"But the plague is in London! Is that not why you left? My dear Mistress Olivia, I cannot believe that the plague is preferable to the court!"

"Then you clearly have no idea how the court and its ways are viewed by most honest Englishmen, my lord."

"I do not care in the least what the prim money-grabbing citizens think of the court — but I would think you very foolish to risk the sickness as a means of escaping the taint of the court. Especially after all that has happened."

"Yes," she said tartly. "It almost made you wish you were a stranger to lust when you thought it had led you to bring the plague under your roof."

He did not reply to that insinuation, and she saw that he was frowning a little.

"The plague is hardly a joking matter, Mistress Paris." He looked down at her. "Have you seen anyone die of it?"

"Once," she replied. "About three weeks ago — a

43

man fell dead in the street quite near to me. But he was lucky to die so easily."

"Very lucky. The thought of such a death is enough to cast a shadow over —" He shivered. "It sets one thinking —"

"You'll be telling me next you've suffered a sudden conversion, my lord," Olivia mocked him, "and that from now on you will lead a reformed and blameless life."

He grinned at her.

"The only time I'm likely to repent of my past misdeeds, Mistress Olivia, is on my deathbed — if then."

"I doubt if that will be soon enough," she retorted.

"A pity — for in that case we're not likely to meet in the afterlife. An eternity of your sweet company — it would be an enticing prospect."

She glanced up to see if he were remotely serious, but his smile was as ironical and uncommunicative as ever.

"I think an eternity of your company would be a just reward for a misspent life," she said sharply.

"Ah, Mistress Olivia, that was not kind!" he returned with a regretful shake of the head.

"I am not inclined to be kind, knowing what I do of you."

"Then I shall shame you now with my unblemished courtesy — what's wrong?" For she had come to a standstill again as they reached the front of the house.

"I don't want to go this way, not through the house. There's a shorter way —"

"You find your memories too painful to contemplate? — Come now, Mistress Olivia, I thought you were made of sterner stuff. Besides, we are here now, and I hoped you'd take some refreshment with me before returning to your duties."

"I have given you no reason to think I would," Olivia rebuffed him. But she allowed him to lead her into the flagged entrance hall. Curiosity drew her on, in spite of her reluctance to face whatever changes he had made.

That there were changes was obvious at once. Rich carpets lay on the floors, the furniture was finer and more elaborate, gilded and embroidered. And the pictures — Olivia felt the colour rush to her cheeks as her eye fell on the vast canvases in the hall, seemingly filled with riotous expanses of naked pink flesh. Her father would not have approved; and nor did she. His taste had been for landscapes and still-lifes, gentle quiet paintings, of which he had made a considerable collection. She wondered what had become of them: everything had been forfeited to the King on his death.

"These weren't here before," she said disapprovingly, her eyes drawn reluctantly to the indecent canvases. It was impossible not to look at them.

"Not to your taste, I see," he observed. "Though I would not have expected them to be. These should be more to your liking." He led her into the beautiful panelled parlour next door, with its lovely plastered ceiling and low windows looking over the garden. She had always loved this room best. And here, fittingly perhaps, her father's tranquil paintings hung, restful and pleasing to the eye. With them were a number of religious works, which Edward Paris would roundly have condemned as idolatrous, but they were distinctly preferable, Olivia thought, to those other horrors.

Once, above the fireplace here, had hung two portraits of her parents. They had gone, as she would have expected, and in their place hung a single portrait of a plain young woman, little more than a girl, fair and serious and looking very uncomfortable in her fashionable low-necked, tight-laced silk gown.

"Who is she?" Olivia asked, pausing before the portrait.

"My wife."

45

She turned sharply.

"Your wife!"

"My late wife, I should have said," he corrected himself. "She died of smallpox soon after we were married." He broke in on the expression of sympathy forming on Olivia's lips. "I didn't shed any tears on her behalf. We had nothing in common, and she brought me a fortune. An admirably considerate wife."

"Poor girl," Olivia murmured, looking up at the unremarkable face. She could not have known much happiness, Olivia suspected. "You had no children then?" she asked next.

"No, unfortunately. It means I shall have to wed again some time, or the Earldom will die with me — an unthinkable prospect. But there's time enough for that. She must be the right lady —"

"And what do you look for in a wife?" asked Olivia with genuine curiosity.

"Oh, land I think this time, if possible. Good birth, of course, and health and strength and the right build for child-bearing. A good devout well-bred little Catholic girl — they make excellent wives. Obedient and uncomplaining. She will stay quietly here and raise my sons and never ask to be taken to court — except when necessary — or complain that she sees too little of me. And she will be dutifully blind to the company I keep at my house in London, or at court."

Olivia shuddered.

"I pity her!" she said fervently. He glanced at her in surprise.

"I cannot think why. She will have Spensley, and a title, and freedom to follow what interests she pleases, so long as they do not conflict with mine. Few wives have as much."

"And what of affection?"

"Oh, that may come perhaps, if she pleases me and I her. But one does not expect it or look for it."

46

Which, Olivia thought sadly, was probably true of very many marriages. At least she was unlikely to have to face that problem. She had nothing with which to tempt a husband.

She turned away from the portrait and began to make her way back towards the hall. William, familiar with the house by now, and tired of the interminable adult conversation, had already set off to rejoin his sisters. Olivia quickened her step hoping to catch him up. But half-way across the hall Lord Alston laid a hand on her arm.

"Come, take a glass of wine with me."

Olivia shook off his hand.

"I must return to the children."

But he had already turned to a small table and poured wine into a glass. Now he handed it to her, smiling.

"You cannot refuse me now," he said confidently. Olivia was strongly tempted to do exactly that. But however much she disliked him, he had, on the whole, behaved generously towards her — and to the children. It would be churlish to refuse a moment more of his company. She took the glass with a polite murmur of thanks.

"To your lovely eyes!" he proposed, raising his glass.

"I don't drink toasts," she said stiffly, and he laughed.

"No, you would not, I suppose. But the toast is mine, sweet Puritan."

She sipped at the wine, watching him warily. He stood by the hearth, one hand resting on the carved overmantel, and looked at her with a sparkle of ironical amusement in his blue eyes. And then all at once he set down his glass and came nearer, suddenly grave again. She recoiled a little as his hand rested on her cheek, and then slid to her shoulder to lie lightly caressing her neck. In spite of herself she felt desire

47

stir within her.

"It is a great pity," he said softly, "that you are — who you are. Otherwise we might have seen very much more of one another in the future."

"What makes you think I have any wish to see any more of you than I have already?" she demanded. He smiled.

"That would have depended on the circumstances — but imagine an establishment of your own in my London house, all you could ask for in the way of clothes, food, furniture and so on — your own coach — dependent on no one but myself, able to live as you please, not always at another's beck and call — any children well cared for —"

With a gasp of indignation Olivia put down her glass and pushed aside his caressing hand.

"You are suggesting —? Oh, how can you!"

He gazed at her with genuine astonishment.

"I do not see why you should be so angry. Most women would think it an honour to be set up as a great man's mistress — in particular, a woman in your unenviable position. But, never fear, it cannot be — it would hardly be a sure path to the King's favour to take the daughter of a regicide as one's mistress. He is a man of great kindness and tolerance, but there are limits."

"For which I can clearly thank God!" she retorted. "Do you really think I would have been tempted for a moment?"

He drained his glass, watching her, and then said: "Yes, I do." And as she began to protest again he drew her suddenly into his arms. Olivia struggled wildly, her hands beating against his chest, but somehow his mouth found hers and all resistance melted from her with dismaying speed. All too soon she had given herself up to the sweetness of his kiss, oblivious to everything but his nearness.

This time, after a short while, he released her, holding her a little way off and looking down at her with eyes darkened by passion.

"I want you, Olivia," he said hoarsely. "It would not hurt to take you now, this once —"

Frustrated passion gave fire to her anger. She reached up and slapped him, sharply, across the face. And then she pulled herself free.

"You disgust me!" she cried violently. And before he could think of anything to say she had run from the room.

Outside the bedroom upstairs Olivia paused and tried to calm herself. She did not want the children to see the deep emotions which must mark her face at the moment. Disgust at the Earl's behaviour, contempt for all he was and all he represented, mingled with shame at her own weakness. Arrogant, hateful man, she thought, to think that any woman must as a matter of course find him utterly irresistible! The fact that the moment his arms closed about her, as soon even as his hand touched her, she did in fact find him precisely that was no consolation at all. How could she be so weak as to be so stirred to passion by a man who was not even remotely worthy of her respect?

But however ashamed she was at the new depths of wantonness he had exposed within her, it was the Earl she blamed above all. No decent man, whatever his feelings, would have set out to seduce a respectable woman, to lure her to a life of immorality, as he today had tried to do. And this time he had not even the excuse of drunkenness! A compassionate man would have seen her lonely, dependent position as an added reason for restraint, not as a useful weapon to employ against her.

The more she knew of Lord Alston, the more he confirmed all that she had heard about the court. And the more convinced she was that even the plague for all its horrors was less dangerous, less evil by far than the world which revolved about the King.

But Olivia had the children to consider, and she did not seriously contemplate returning to London, even for a moment. Her one aim now must be to help Barbara quickly back to health so that they could go on their way to Oxford. Once there, she knew there was little likelihood that she need be troubled by the court, any more than she was in London when the King was at Whitehall. The Earl himself had pointed out that hers was a name unlikely ever to be welcome at court, and even her brother and his wife did not move in such elevated circles, however much they might have regretted it.

As she turned the handle and pushed open the door Olivia resolved that she would devote herself to Barbara and make sure that her own path did not cross with Lord Alston's again before the child was fit to leave Spensley.

For over a week Olivia found no difficulty in keeping to her resolve. Through the day she sat with Barbara in the bedroom, caring for her, talking to her, amusing her. When the child grew strong enough to benefit from the fresh air, Olivia carried her down to the garden and sat with her in some sheltered corner from which she had a good view of anyone approaching along the paths. If she saw the Earl coming that way, she gathered Barbara up in her arms and beat a hurried retreat up the short flight of stairs to their room.

After the first few days the child began to recover quickly, better than Olivia had feared she might. Before long she was able to walk about the room, even down the stairs, and then to join briefly in the games of the other children. She was almost well enough, Olivia thought triumphantly, to face the journey to Oxford.

She was standing in the garden one day watching

the children playing at ball, and so deep in the happy prospect of leaving Spensley that she forgot temporarily to watch for the approach of her detested host. He was at her side, speaking so suddenly that she jumped, before she even knew he was near.

"I've found you at last, Mistress Olivia!" he said with satisfaction. "You have become singularly elusive of late."

"Did you not believe me when I said I had no desire at all for your company?" she retorted, when she had controlled herself enough to speak. His sudden appearance had overturned all her serenity in a moment. She felt flustered and breathless and trembling, and she knew she had blushed deeply. His next words did not help, either.

"No desire at all?" he asked, so pointedly that she had to bend her head so he could not read the confusion in her eyes.

"Why don't you leave me alone?" she demanded.

"It would hardly be courteous," he returned lightly. "You are my guest, after all."

"Most unwillingly," she pointed out, and then wished the words unsaid. After all, with Barbara sick as she was their plight would have been appalling, unthinkable, had he not come on them that morning on the road. Ashamed of herself, more confused than ever, she raised her eyes to his face. "I'm sorry," she said contritely. "That was churlish of me."

She regretted her apology the next moment, when he bent and kissed her lightly on the lips. If only that treacherous part of herself did not wish that the kiss had been very much more prolonged!

He took her arm and slid it through his own, laying his other hand over hers. It was warm, and strong, completely covering her own, and she tried not to admit even to herself how much she liked the feel of it.

"I have something for you," he said next. She

51

looked up at him questioningly. "Something I remembered the other day — come with me."

She pulled her hand free, and shook her head.

"I'm not leaving the children," she said stubbornly.

"Don't be foolish — and I have them just in here — it's not far. Come and look through the window at least."

She went with him then, and looked through a window close by, into a small room which her father had used as a study. Evidently the Earl made some similar use of it, though there was nothing to show that he spent much of his time in it. And there, propped against a table, stood the two portraits which had hung once above the parlour fire.

"Oh!" she cried, involuntarily. She was dimly aware that the Earl had put his arm about her shoulders, but all her attention was on the pictures.

"You may have them," he told her softly. "I think by rights they are yours in any case. I can have them sent to London, once you return there — if that's what you'd like."

She looked up at him, her face rosy, but with pleasure this time.

"Thank you, my lord — I am most deeply grateful."

"They're no use to me," he returned casually, letting his arm fall and moving to lean against the wall beyond the window. "You might as well have them. They've been gathering dust in the attics since I came home — I'd meant to have them destroyed, but had forgotten about them."

His words effectively cooled her gratitude, but could not completely quell it. After she had gazed through the window again for a little longer, he said suddenly,

"You were fond of your father weren't you?"

"Yes," she said. "I loved him very dearly. And my mother too. Does that surprise you?"

He shrugged.

"I have nothing to judge the matter by. I never knew my own father. Or my mother, come to that."

She looked up at him.

"Who brought you up?"

He shrugged again.

"This person and that. My mother was one of the Queen's ladies, so I was brought up at her court in France. I had nursemaids, of course, and tutors, and the ladies made a great fuss of me. I expect I was greatly over-indulged."

Olivia regarded him thoughtfully. The Queen of whom he spoke was, she supposed, Henrietta Maria, French Catholic wife of King Charles the First and mother of their present King: also, many thought, a wholly disastrous influence upon her husband. Olivia had a vivid mental picture of the pretty blond orphan pampered and fussed over in that self-centred, intriguing court-in-exile. Pampered, yet unloved. She felt a sudden unexpected pity for him.

"It must have been very lonely," she commented after a moment.

It was clearly the last thing he had thought she would say. He glanced at her in astonishment; and then he said abruptly, as if he was surprised himself to realise that it was true: "Yes, it was."

After that he turned away and began to walk back towards the children. Olivia left the window and followed him.

"My lord," she said, as she reached his side. "Barbara is much better now. I think it is time we went on to Oxford."

At that he halted, and gave a little bow.

"Certainly, Mistress Paris. I had intended to travel to court the day after tomorrow. I shall be pleased to accommodate you in my coach." The stiff formality of his manner startled her almost as much as his immediate turning away from her to stride quickly along the grassy paths to the front of the house. But

53

Olivia's strongest emotion as she watched him go was one of relief that very soon she could take her leave of him for ever.

FOUR

The Earl of Alston behaved with the utmost correctness on the short journey to Oxford. There was no hint in his manner towards Olivia of irony, or of hidden meanings designed to embarrass her. For much of the time he did not talk at all, but sat gazing out of the window at the passing countryside, already tinted with autumn. When he did speak it was to address some general and inoffensive remark to her, on the weather, or the state of the roads. Once, he spoke of her father's collection of paintings, and how he liked them; and once of music, of which she had little knowledge or appreciation. But always his tone was cool, unemotional, courteous yet a little bored. He even exerted himself to talk to the children, but rather in the manner of a man who had no experience at all of dealing with the young. His chilly courtesy made Olivia feel a little uncomfortable.

He was a strange man, she reflected once, watching him while his attention was centred on some apparently uninteresting scene beyond the window. She had supposed him incapable of seriousness, in speech or thought, except when frightened into it by fear of the plague. So often, hearing him talk, she had felt herself shut out from any understanding of him by his light teasing manner. Yet today, when there was no hint of that lightness, she felt if anything that she was seeing even less of the man beneath that splendid façade. She wondered, with her eyes on his magnificent profile, what kind of man he really was. Superficial, cynical and amoral, incapable of any depth of thought or feeling: so she supposed. But she was not sure.

After all, he had sheltered them at Spensley when most men would have driven them away.

She was no nearer to finding an answer to the puzzle when the coach drew to a halt before the pleasant unimpressive house on the edge of Oxford where Henry's friends lived.

"Here we are, Mistress Paris," said the Earl with audible satisfaction. "You cannot be said to have come here by the quickest or the most direct route, but you have reached your destination at last. And now we must part."

"And I must thank you for your hospitality," she returned, matching his distant politeness of tone. She felt obscurely hurt that he should show so little warmth, when until today he had almost shown too much. But, after all, she had not welcomed his troublesome approaches in the past. It was hardly logical to mind that he behaved more coolly towards her now: she ought to be thankful for it.

For a moment he took her hand and bent his head to kiss it. But his touch was as light and passionless as if she had been an elderly and ill-favoured gentlewoman to whom he owed the minimum of respect. He did not even smile as the footman came to open the door of the coach and help Olivia and the children to the ground.

"Goodbye, my lord, and thank you," said Olivia as she stood with the children beside the modest front porch of the house. The Earl bowed his head.

"Goodbye, Mistress Paris," was his only reply before the door was closed upon him and the coach moved off.

The Earl gave one last enigmatic glance at the little group, and then leaned his head back and closed his eyes and gave a great sigh of relief. At least, he reflected thankfully, he had finally succeeded in extricating himself from an uncomfortable situation with some measure of dignity. He knew that until today that had been far from the truth. Never again, he resolved, would he take up a young woman on the whim of a moment: it could so easily have been a fatal impulse. And then, even knowing who she was, he had found himself making the most unwise of advances to her. The thought was the more humiliating in that she had rejected those advances so very forcibly. He had been a fool even to imagine he could make any progress with her, the more especially when he had not really wanted to do so, once he knew her identity. Though she had responded to him, like tinder to the flame —

Abruptly, he brushed that thought aside. After all, he was well accustomed to finding himself attractive to women. If she had answered his passion more ardently than most, it did not alter the outcome. She was a young woman who could have brought him nothing but disaster, and had indeed very nearly done so. He was well rid of her.

Now, he thought with a smile of satisfaction, for a return to the congenial company of his own kind. To the King whom he served, and the court in which he was most at home, and its women. Women like the beautiful Mistress Cunningham, whose complaisant husband was a minor court official; and Moll Simpson, the pretty actress, temporarily agreeably idle while the theatres were closed. With them he knew exactly where he stood.

As soon as Olivia and the children were admitted to the parlour where Celia sat with her friend and hostess, Mistress Elizabeth Weston, Olivia knew that her worst fears had been well-founded: Celia was very far from delighted to see her children standing alive and well before her.

For a moment, their mother gazed at the children with her pretty pink and white face temporarily devoid of colour, and her eyes wide and frightened.

The plump hands which stroked the little dog crouching on her lap were visibly trembling. She raised her light blue eyes to Olivia's grave face.

"What does this mean?" she demanded sharply. "Why have you come?"

"Because Mr Benson's house was shut up with the plague, and I thought you would wish me to bring the children to safety," returned Olivia with quiet firmness.

Celia's hand flew to her breast.

"Mr Benson's house? Next door?" It seemed scarcely possible, but Olivia thought Celia grew still paler. And visibly, though they were seated and she herself was standing, the two older women drew in their skirts and recoiled from the little group of new arrivals. "But you may have brought the sickness here!"

It was not the moment to mention Barbara's illness. Olivia simply shook her head and said calmly: "We have been more than a week on our way. If we were infected I think the sickness would have shown itself by now."

"But the plague has even reached the countryside, so we are told. There are even fears that it may come this far!"

"We have not been near anyone with the sickness, Celia," Olivia assured her. "You will take no risk in welcoming your children. Only, they themselves will be safe."

Celia ran doubtful eyes over the three silent figures gazing at her with all the solemnity of near-strangers.

"But what am I to do with you all?" she pondered with a little frown. Olivia glanced towards Celia's hostess: the fleeting expression caught on the other woman's face was not encouraging. It was quite clear that Elizabeth Weston was utterly dismayed at the probability that she would have to welcome Celia's children and their aunt. It occurred to Olivia that perhaps Celia and Henry had already outstayed their

58

welcome.

"If only we had a little more room, I should be only too happy to . . ." began Mistress Weston, but before she could complete the sentence Celia had broken effusively in.

"My dear Betty, you are so very kind! It is a dreadful imposition, I know, when you have already borne with our company for so long, but it is delightful that we can always depend so on your generosity! Though your house is small, your heart is indeed large. My children will remember your hospitality with gratitude, when they are full grown."

Once, Elizabeth went so far as to protest faintly, "But . . .!" before she was overcome by the flood of Celia's outpouring. By the time her guest had finished Elizabeth's eyes held a defeated look, depressed yet resigned. Her mouth tight with disapproval she rose to call servants to make an attic room ready for the new arrivals, but showing very plainly how little she wanted them. Olivia wondered if Celia had any sensitivity at all, to be so oblivious to her hostess's dismay. Though she had never thought sensitivity one of Celia's qualities, except where her own comfort was concerned.

Not even at Spensley, where it seemed that she might have brought the plague, had she felt so unwelcome, Olivia reflected, as she trudged behind the broad back of a servant up apparently interminable stairs towards the small bleak room beneath the roof which she was to share with the children. Here a tiny window let in the minimum of light, and revealed two truckle beds and a chest to be the sole furnishings. There would not in any case have been room for anything else. It was not a cheering prospect.

It was clear that the cramped bedroom was only one indication as to how deeply the arrival of Olivia and the children was resented. Mistress Weston had been prevented by Celia from refusing to take them in at all, but in no other way was she willing to pretend that she was glad to have them. In any case, thought Olivia, very likely she knew that so long as she was not forced to suffer any discomfort herself as a consequence, Celia did not mind at all how her sister-in-law and the children were treated. They were almost as much of a nuisance to herself as they were to her hostess.

So when Olivia and the children were despatched to eat with the servants in the kitchen, and excluded from all the activities of the Westons themselves — from rides and walks, dancing and music and long hours of conversation at the fireside — Celia made no objection at all. If anything, Olivia suspected, she was glad to be able to forget that they were there. It was Olivia who played with the children in the pleasant garden, and told them stories, and washed and dressed them, and comforted them when they were hurt. But as that had always been her role, even in London, it was nothing new, and she did not mind. And as for eating in the kitchen, she suspected that the company there was probably both more congenial and more lively than that in parlour and dining room.

Henry she saw even less than his wife. When they met for the first time after her arrival he gave her a perfunctory greeting, with no hint of thanks for her care of his children, and then, like his wife, appeared to forget she was there.

Of one thing Olivia quickly became very sure: Henry and Celia had overstayed their welcome a long time ago. Every word and expression of their hosts marked their impatience to be rid of their guests. And in the kitchen it was openly acknowledged that the Warriners could not leave soon enough for the peace of the household. It was a joke that even the broadest hint, verging on rudeness, seemed to go unnoticed by the thick-skinned pair.

John Weston had been a childhood friend of Henry

Warriner, but he had done well enough for himself to buy a small estate and set himself up in comfort there. Any liking between the two men had largely gone now, in particular after three months of daily company. But Henry and Celia were comfortable at Oxford, and well away from the plague, and they had no intention of leaving until London was safe again.

That, now, they had an added reason for staying where they were Olivia was soon to learn. Not that either Celia or Henry went so far as to confide in her; but as Celia returned one day from an excursion into the city, Olivia heard her telling Elizabeth Weston how she had glimpsed the King himself, walking with a group of courtiers and ladies, amongst them his favourite mistress, Lady Castlemaine. With a little smirk, Celia patted her fair curls.

"I fancied once he looked my way," she added confidingly. Olivia was astonished that she seemed unaware of the contemptuous look which her hostess cast upon her.

"You and I and people of our kind would be wise to avoid any contact with the court," said Elizabeth Weston stiffly.

"Ah, but if Henry could make a name for himself — even as a supplier of wines —" Celia retorted. "Many men have been made by the court."

"And many women unmade," her friend reminded her tartly.

So, thought Olivia, watching the two women as they walked away together, Celia and Henry hoped to gain some small influence at court, some foothold to prosperity. She felt almost pitying at so hopeless an aspiration. But it was hard to feel genuine pity in the face of such foolishness. Even in a city as small and enclosed as Oxford it was unlikely that two commonplace Londoners would have any chance of entering the world of the court. Celia might have a certain plump prettiness, but she had no other qualities with

61

which to catch the King's eye, if that was what she hoped. And there was not likely to be any other way open to the Warriners of gaining access to such dizzy influence. Olivia was very glad that she had little to do with Celia and Henry now. If that was what filled their minds, then the further she kept herself from it the better.

After that, Olivia found herself wondering briefly what Celia would have said had she known where her sister-in-law had stayed on her journey to Oxford. But she had said nothing to Celia, and naturally Celia had not asked. So it might have remained, had not Celia said suddenly one day: "Barbara looks a little thin."

The children had been playing in the garden while their mother walked in the autumn sun. Further away, Henry and John Weston played at bowls.

"That's because of her illness," said Paulina solemnly. "But she's much better now."

Olivia's heart gave a great lurch. What would Celia say now? Worse still, what would Paulina tell her?

"Illness?" Celia demanded sharply, with more real interest in her children's concern than she had shown since their arrival. "What illness is that?" She glanced at Olivia, as if expecting her to answer.

"Barbara was unwell on our way here," replied Olivia slowly.

"But a kind gentleman gave us shelter in his house," added Paulina, to Olivia's alarm. She prayed fervently that in Celia's imagination the 'kind gentleman' would take the shape of someone sober and elderly. It would not be easy to answer if the questions became more pressing. But she should have remembered how little curious Celia was about the doings of her children and their aunt. It was beyond her imagination to suspect that anything which happened to them could be of any real interest or significance. Only when it might affect her could it merit her attention. And now only the fact that

Barbara had been ill seemed of any importance.

"How was she unwell? What was wrong? Why did you not tell me?" Her eyes were wide with alarm.

"I did not think you would wish to be worried," replied Olivia quietly. "Particularly as she recovered so well."

"It wasn't the plague," put in Paulina. That, Olivia saw, was the reassurance which Celia demanded. Once sure of that fact, Barbara's mother lost all interest in her child's recent illness. She called to her little dog — more like a large and yapping powder puff than a dog, Olivia often thought — and wandered away to watch her husband's game.

During her first weeks in Oxford Olivia rarely left the confines of the house and garden. Once, she went to church, but she missed the austere worship she was accustomed to enjoy in London, where those of her non-conformist beliefs had to meet in secret, for fear of the law, and she declined to go again. It was the only point on which she openly defied her brother and his wife, for they thought her refusal to conform deeply shocking.

"With your name you can't be too careful," Henry had said to her, soon after she came to live with them in London. To which she had replied that she was proud of her name and intended to worship as she felt inclined. Freedom to follow what religion one chose had been one of her father's most deeply held principles. She used to feel almost as if he were at her side when she walked through the London streets on Sundays to the merchant's house where those who thought as she did met for worship. But here in Oxford she did not know where to go to find such kindred spirits: perhaps there were none in this traditionally Royalist city.

Of the court and its activities Olivia was relieved to find that she saw nothing at all. Her daily life revolved around the children and their needs. She did not even need to go shopping, as she was no longer in her own home. It was easy to forget that beyond the quiet garden and the comfortable house the colleges and streets echoed with the songs and laughter, the music and the quarrels of innumerable courtiers. And that among them, somewhere, a tall gentleman bent his fair head attentively towards a beautiful lady, or led his partner into the dance.

Olivia was surprised at how often, in spite of all she knew of him, her thoughts went to the Earl, how often she wondered where he was, or what he was doing. It was not, she told herself, that she was remotely interested in the answer. She did not even want to know in what depraved way he passed his time. She was quite certain she would not approve of it. Perhaps it was because he was now the owner of Spensley that he came to mind so often. If so, she must try not to think of him, for that part of her life was over now and could never come again. She must live in the present.

The longer she stayed in Oxford, the more sure Olivia became that the Westons' patience was growing daily closer to breaking point. What brought matters to a head at last she did not know; but she was in the attic room one morning late in October hearing the children at their lessons when Celia burst in.

Olivia could not remember ever having seen her sister-in-law so distraught. Her plump prettiness was in wild disorder, her large empty blue eyes rimmed with red from crying, her self-centred composure totally overthrown. She stood in the doorway, lip quivering, saying nothing, and Olivia set the children some work to do and rose quietly to her feet, taking Celia by the elbow and steering her from the room. As soon as the door closed behind them Celia dissolved into helpless tears. Olivia laid an arm about her shoulders.

"Come now, Celia, don't cry — what's the matter?"

Jerkily, between sobs, the story emerged. Some chance remark of Celia's — she could not remember what — had stung Elizabeth to anger. She had said something unpardonable in reply. And from that a fierce quarrel had ensued, in the course of which Elizabeth had declared roundly that if Celia and Henry were to leave now it would not be a moment too soon, and that even the plague would be easier to bear than two such trying guests.

Olivia patted Celia's shoulder, mildly relieved that at least the children's presence did not seem to have been an added bone of contention. Apart from that, she could not help feeling deeply sympathetic towards the Westons. Yet on the other hand to Celia and Henry it must seem impossible to contemplate returning to London and the threat of the plague, and they had nowhere else to go.

"Put on your cloak, and we'll go for a walk," Olivia advised at last. "That often helps to make things seem better." Fresh air was a great clearer of the head, she had always thought.

So they set out together in the crisp autumn sunlight, walking steadily in no particular direction, and with Celia still hiccoughing miserably from time to time.

"What can we do?" she cried at last, when they had progressed in silence for a little while.

"I heard it said in the kitchen yesterday that deaths of the plague in London had lessened by about six hundred last week," Olivia observed thoughtfully.

"And how many did die, all the same?" demanded Celia pointedly. "The deaths are still in the thousands, are they not?" Olivia nodded. "Then how can we go home?" her sister-in-law went on, drawing out her handkerchief and dabbing her eyes. "We would risk our very lives."

'Only as you were prepared to risk those of your children,' thought Olivia severely. But it was hardly the moment to apportion blame. Instead, she said: "Can you not find lodgings in the town here? Or in a safer part of London?"

Celia shook her head.

"How can we? They charge so much for a few rooms in these hard times."

"Then the only thing you can do, as I see it, is to ask Mistress Weston's pardon for offending her, and tell her that as soon as the plague lessens a little further you will go home. Surely, when winter comes, it must grow less?"

"I don't know," returned Celia dejectedly.

They walked a little further in silence, and then took a narrow lane towards Christ Church meadow. Olivia had not consciously chosen this route, but now they were here she thought it might after all be a very good thing. If they were by chance to catch a glimpse or two of King or courtiers, nothing would be better calculated than that to cheer Celia out of her present misery. And the King himself was lodged within the ancient walls of Christ Church College.

The meadow stretched tranquil and golden green from the boundaries of the colleges which skirted it to the banks of the river. And there, sure enough, near the river's edge, stood a colourful group of gentlemen and ladies, splendidly dressed, their laughter and high spirited talk carrying over the meadow towards the two women. A glance at Celia told Olivia that the older woman had already brightened a little.

The group at the waterside turned and began to make their way, slowly and with many pauses, punctuated by shouts and laughter, in their direction.

"Perhaps the King himself is there," murmured Celia eagerly, her hand busy smoothing her hair as she narrowed her eyes the better to see. Olivia, whose eyesight was keener, was reasonably certain that the King was not one of the group. She knew that he was taller than most men, lean and very dark. One man did indeed stand a head taller than his companions, but his hair was fair, golden fair, its shining curls bright in the sun —

Olivia stood still, her heart leaping painfully. Her chief impulse was to turn and flee towards the protection of the streets. Walking here, they must almost inevitably meet, unless she could steer Celia in the opposite direction, and that seemed hardly likely, knowing her sister-in-law as she did.

The Earl had a lady on his arm, a lovely creature with copper-coloured hair and a light green gown, who gazed up at him with limpid adoration in her green eyes. He for his part walked with head bent attentively towards her, the teasing lightness of his conversation reflected in his expression. Olivia could almost imagine she heard every word, for did she not know herself how he would talk to a lady? Now, she did turn away, an inexplicable pain tightening about her heart. She felt Celia's hand grasping her arm.

"Olivia, where are you going? Come back — I want to go this way."

"I think it's going to rain," said Olivia, clutching at the first excuse which came into her head. Celia gazed up in bewilderment at the cloudless sky.

"I don't see how you can think that," she retorted. She pouted a little, sulkily. "I want to go this way," she repeated. A tearful note was already creeping into her voice again.

Olivia felt too confused to be able to think of any further reason to deprive Celia of her confrontation with the approaching group. 'Besides,' she thought, 'why should I mind? He is nothing to me, and never was very much more than a tiresome intruder into my life.' She swallowed hard, and allowed Celia to turn her round to face them, even to lead her a little further on over the grass.

They were much nearer now, only a few yards away. And in a moment or two he had seen her. She saw him raise his head, glance their way, and then, his smile fading, break off in mid-sentence, suddenly standing very still. He had gone rather pale. His eyes seemed to hold Olivia's, grave and enigmatic.

He was silent long enough for his companion to tug at his arm, seeking his attention. And then, his face as rosy now as once it had been pale, he removed his hat and gave a little bow in Olivia's direction. After that, he drew the lady's arm more firmly through his own and stepped aside, passing Olivia and Celia without another glance. As they passed, Olivia heard the red-haired lady say brightly:

"What a stiff little Puritan that dark girl looks. A most unbecoming hat, don't you think?"

Olivia stood gazing after them. 'It is strange,' she thought: 'he seemed almost as embarrassed as I. Yet there was no reason for either of us to be troubled at meeting like this. It was not so very unlikely that we should meet some time.' Perhaps he was regretting that he had ever sought her acquaintance. After all, beside that bright creature in green, Olivia Paris was a sober and unappealing prospect. Perhaps he was wondering what he had ever seen in her.

As they walked slowly on towards the river Olivia felt suddenly depressed, as if that uncomfortable encounter had taken some of the brightness from the day. But at her side Celia was transformed, sparkling with delight.

"That was Lord Alston, the King's great friend Lord Alston!" she cried happily. "And he raised his hat to me!"

FIVE

When they reached home, Celia and Olivia found that their hostess had apparently thought better of her outburst of this morning. She made no apology, and certainly did not refer to anything she had said, but she greeted them with courtesy and more concern than usual for their needs. She even invited Olivia to join herself and Celia for cakes and wine in the parlour. For Celia's sake, Olivia hoped that the Westons' almost superhuman patience would last a little longer.

As for herself, she realised very soon that the encounter on Christ Church meadow had unsettled her far more than its significance merited. She was angry with herself that she could still be so easily disturbed by Lord Alston, and this time with no reason at all. She would not, she determined, go wandering in the town again. Her place was at home, with the children, who had become very bored this morning without her.

November brought wind and rain, and Olivia and the children grew tired of spending long wearisome hours in their cramped room with little to do. When a cold grey morning dawned without rain, Olivia declared a day free of lessons and took the children down to the garden.

She wandered slowly along the narrow paths while the children ran shouting and laughing and revelling in freedom and fresh air. She was glad to be out of doors herself, but she could not share their feeling of release. Today, as so often lately, she wondered sadly what life had in store for her. The very best she could hope for, she thought, was that she might continue to care for Henry's children until they in their

69

turn had children of their own. But it was not much of a prospect.

'The best part of my life is over,' she reflected. 'It came to an end when the King came home. Now there is only survival left, the need to endure what comes with patience and courage.' At least she had a roof over her head, somewhere she could call a home, which was more than many orphaned and penniless girls could hope for. Without that her plight would be pitiable indeed.

"I seem doomed to find you always surrounded by children," came a voice at her elbow.

Olivia turned, sharply, with a little cry; and for a moment the garden spun about her.

"My lord!" she breathed. She struggled to control herself, and then said, her face fiery red, "What are you doing here?"

She was reminded instantly of that meeting in Christ Church meadow, for the Earl looked even more uncomfortable and unsure of himself than she was herself. The mocking assurance of his manner seemed to have disappeared under some unaccountable emotion. His smile now was uncertain, hesitant.

"I came to see you, of course," he replied, with a poor echo of the confident tone she had grown used to hearing, to her constant irritation.

"But why?" she demanded. He made a helpless gesture with his hands.

"I don't know." He began to move on along the path, and she walked with him, puzzled and intrigued. "I found a side door to the garden," he confessed, "and came in on impulse. I thought I might find you."

She gazed at him in amazement at such inexplicable behaviour, and he caught her eye and smiled ruefully.

"I suppose I was bored," he suggested. That seemed the only possible explanation, though it was hardly flattering to Olivia to see herself simply as a last resort in moments of boredom. But then she did not

70

want to have even so much importance to this man.

She realised when they had walked on in silence for a little way that they had turned a corner into the orchard, cut off by a high wall from where the children were playing, their voices still distantly audible. She felt a tremor of alarm: she had learned to her cost that it was unwise to be alone with the Earl.

"I ought to stay with the children," she said hastily. Lord Alston turned towards her, and she saw from his eyes that her fears had been amply justified. Before she could move away his hand had slid into her hair and drawn her towards him, and she found herself held in that relentless embrace. His mouth came to hers, hungrily, as if he had been starved for want of her through the past weeks, firm, demanding, full of passion. She resisted only for an instant before reaching up to hold him, to spread her fingers in the warm thickness of his hair, to press her body to his, stirred by the hard lines of bone and muscle against her. Somewhere, deep within her, a small voice cried: 'I have so little — why should I not have this?' The guilt and shame she would know afterwards would be nothing set against the sweetness of his kiss upon her parted lips, his hands seeking her breasts beneath the concealing gorget.

After a while he drew away, cupping her face in his hands and gazing down at her through narrowed eyes.

"'What's in a name?'" he murmured hoarsely. "'A rose by any other name would smell as sweet'."

Olivia felt as if two fierce emotions warred within her: desire, for him to take her in his arms; anger, that he should once more have taken advantage of her feelings. The one prompted her to reach out to draw him to her; the other, to jerk herself free and walk quickly back to the children. In fact she did neither, only stood there with her heart beating fast and her lips parted as he went on:

"Could you not take your brother's name? Then you could be mine — my own Mistress Olivia."

'My own mistress' — as Lady Castlemaine was the King's, as so many women of all kinds were to the gentlemen of the court. All at once it was as if the sweetness of this moment, alone with him among the autumn scents of decaying leaves, and woodsmoke, and the dying year, had been tainted, darkened by the shadow of that corrupt world outside. Just now in his arms she had not felt that it had been like that, ugly and sordid and dirty; but now she saw it for what it was. It was easy now to shake her head free and draw away, eyes bright and hard as ebony.

"I am proud of my name," she said coldly. "I have no wish to bring it to dishonour." And then she turned away and found herself face to face with Celia, coming to seek her on some errand.

She stood very still, face glowing with embarrassment, and wondering painfully how long her sister-in-law had been there. What had she seen? She looked as if she had just rounded the corner, but one could not be sure. She herself had been so very far from knowing what was happening outside that little space where she stood with the Earl.

Whatever Celia had seen — and Olivia began to think it could not have been much — it was the Earl's presence now which caught her attention. She gazed past Olivia, and dropped a little curtsey, and bestowed her most simpering smile on the young man who frowned down at her from his great height.

"My lord — you do us great honour by coming here!"

Olivia glanced over her shoulder at Lord Alston, noting how he struggled to control himself, how he made a move as if to call after her, and then thought better of it and turned a chilly smile upon her sister-in-law.

'She's welcome to him!' thought Olivia, and left

them together. Married or not, Celia would be per-
fectly willing to allow a man influential at court to
lure her to his bed. It did not make her feel any more
kindly towards Celia. Better the beautiful redhead
than her silly, selfish sister-in-law. She wondered
whether he would be tempted.

It was much later in the day, as she emerged from
supper in the kitchen, that Celia waylaid her and drew
her into the deserted parlour. Olivia's eyes searched
her face for any indication as to what had happened
in the garden this morning, but could read nothing
out of the ordinary there, no excitement or elation,
though clearly Celia had something on her mind.

"I learned this morning," she declared at last, "that
my lord Alston came here to see you."

"Oh?" returned Olivia, as casually as she could.
"Did he say so?"

"Indeed he did — and made it plain that you had
met before!"

Olivia bent her head, gazing down at her linked
hands.

"Oh," she said uncomfortably.

"When was that?"

So he had not spoken of her stay at Spensley. For
that at least she was thankful.

"Once, some time ago. It doesn't matter. It was
not important."

"Not important! Olivia, he is a friend of the King!"

Olivia turned to look out of the window.

"What difference does that make? Except to tar
him with the same brush as his master. You know
what I think of the court."

New excitement was clear in Celia's tone.

"Olivia, the court is the way to all prosperity and
influence — think, think what it could mean if we
were to gain a foothold there!"

"That is your business, not mine," retorted Olivia
with a shrug.

"But Lord Alston has his eye on you — he would like you as his mistress."

Olivia turned, white-faced.

"Did he tell you *that*?"

"Not in so many words. But it was clear enough. He expressed a wish to call on you again."

"Then I hope you told him we do not want any further acquaintance with his kind."

"Of course I did not." Celia took her arm and led her to a chair. "Olivia, just think what it could mean —!"

Olivia stood still beside the chair and fixed her sister-in-law with a look of grave severity.

"What *what* could mean?" she asked. Celia had the grace to avoid her eyes as she replied.

"If . . . if you were to become the . . . mistress . . . of a great courtier . . ."

Angrily Olivia shook the hand from her arm.

"God forgive you, Celia, because I won't! How could you even suggest such a thing?"

"It is a great honour to be chosen by a man high at court. He is an Earl, Olivia, and very rich — and young and handsome too. And you are alone in the world — and Henry and I would be so happy to see you well established."

"So that you can rise on my ruin? No thank you, Celia. My father did not raise me to be a whore."

"I wouldn't call it that!" protested Celia, a little shocked.

"Wouldn't you? What would you call it then?" Olivia turned back to the window. "Make no mistake, Celia: to me, for any woman to allow herself to be used like that, as a man's plaything — however rich and powerful the man — even if it is the King himself — that is to submit to the deepest degradation. And I would not consider it for a moment."

"Then you're a fool!" retorted Celia, in a momentary burst of real anger. Almost at once, she was calm

74

again, her voice coaxing. "Come, Olivia, don't be so prim — and think of all we have done for you! Do you not want to repay us for sheltering you all these years? After all, it was not to our advantage to do so, was it, considering who you are?"

"And that is the very reason why I could not seriously be of interest to any courtier," Olivia pointed out, hoping that logic might succeed where appeals to principle clearly had not. "Do you not see that?"

"Has not Henry often urged you to take his name? No one then would connect you with your father."

"I am proud to be connected with my father."

Celia gave a sharp exclamation.

"Stiff-necked, ungrateful girl! I wonder sometimes why we ever troubled to take you in. You have brought us nothing but anxiety and an extra mouth to feed."

"And saved you a good deal in wages for a nursemaid," Olivia reminded her with asperity.

"That's little enough — and now you have it in your power to do us real good."

"Nonsense!" said Olivia briskly. "You have no reason at all to think Lord Alston has any real interest in me — even supposing I was willing to indulge him — which I am not."

"Why else would he come to see you — and be coming again tomorrow?"

Olivia turned appalled eyes upon her.

"Tomorrow!" Celia nodded, smiling a little with satisfaction. "You had no business to permit it without asking me!"

"Why not? You are under age, and Henry and I are responsible for you."

"Then God help me!" cried Olivia despairingly. She had a sudden fleeting sense that she had never in all her life been so alone. Then she said: "But I shall not see him. You cannot force me to do so. If you are so anxious to secure his influence, then charm him yourself."

Celia coloured a little.

"So I should, and gladly," she confessed. "I am
not so cold as to be heedless of his charm – but . . .
it's you he wants, Olivia, though God knows why.
You cannot even dress prettily. If you would learn
the arts to win a man –"

"I don't *want* to win a man – not such a man in
such a way – Why can't you see that, Celia? In any
case," she added, "when have you ever cared what I
wore?"

Celia ran a critical eye over Olivia's dark gown, the
white folds of the gorget, the neat lace-trimmed coif
which concealed her hair. She tried to imagine her
companion dressed as she herself was, in a rose-
coloured gown whose low rounded neck set off her
white breast to perfection, her hair knotted behind,
allowing ringlets to fall on either side of her face. Yes,
in the hands of a good dressmaker – or a kindly
sister-in-law – Olivia might almost hope to lay claim
to beauty.

"Perhaps," she admitted slowly, "I ought to have
given your appearance a little more of my time. But
it is not too late."

"I have no wish to be dressed up like a doll simply
to lure a man I want never to see again. So when he
comes tomorrow you may tell him to go away, and
stay away. He will be wasting his time else."

Celia sniffed and tossed her head.

"We shall see when tomorrow comes," was all she
would say.

The next morning Olivia emerged from the attic
room only to take an early breakfast, and for the rest
of the time kept the children busy at their lessons,
ignoring longing looks directed towards the sunlight
filtering through the small window.

It was late in the morning when a servant came

panting up the stairs to tell her that Mistress Warriner wished to see her in the parlour.

"Please tell Mistress Warriner that I shall be occupied with the children's lessons for some hours yet," Olivia told her. Celia would hardly send Lord Alston up here to find her, she reflected — and nor was he likely to carry his pursuit of her to such lengths.

But Olivia had reckoned without Celia's determination, and without the force of whatever warped emotion had brought the Earl here today. There was scarcely time for the servant to carry her message to Celia before Lord Alston himself appeared in the doorway, with Celia at his elbow.

"Come, children," said their mother, holding out her hands. For a moment the children hesitated, glancing from her face to Olivia's and back again. Olivia longed to contradict Celia's order, but she could not do it: it was not her place to teach them to disobey their mother, whatever her reasons for giving the order. She bent her head, avoiding their questioning eyes, and heard them quietly follow their mother from the room. And then she heard the door close.

She did not look up. She did not need to do so to know that the Earl stood there still, watching her from beside that closed door. But she rose from her seat on one of the hard little beds and stood pretending to look out of the small high window. In reality her eyes saw nothing but his face and its mocking smile. She hoped he could not see how much she was trembling.

"I must ask you to leave, my lord," she said stiffly. "I told Celia I did not wish to see you."

She waited for his teasing reply, and was astonished when he said abruptly:

"Is this where you sleep?"

Something in his tone startled her into turning to look at him. There was no irony in his face, not even a smile. If anything he looked almost a little shocked.

"Yes," she said. "What of it? This is not a large house, and we were not expected."

His eyes ran over the unpolished boards of the floor, the unevenly plastered walls, the uncomfortable beds, the roughly made chest, the inadequate window.

"Is this how you are lodged in London?"

"No," she replied briefly. She thought he seemed almost angry. Certainly he was frowning a little.

"And do you always give the children their lessons, or do they have someone else to do it at home — a tutor, or their mother?"

"No," said Olivia. "I teach them. But I like to do so."

The Earl moved towards her, prodding the straw-filled mattress on one of the beds with a disdainful brown finger.

"And you try to pretend you are not tempted by what I offer you?" he asked, with a wry smile.

"I cannot remember that you offered me anything remotely tempting," she returned coolly.

"An escape from this — from being neither mistress nor servant, but a slave to any unkind whim of your brother and his wife —"

Olivia raised grave eyes to his face.

"My lord, I may not feel that the life I lead at present is in all respects as I would wish it to be; but I can live under my brother's roof and still be myself. That, I think, is better far than to subject my body to the whim of an idle courtier."

He coloured slightly.

"Do you think I should misuse you?"

"I do not wish to be used at all."

He stretched his hands imploringly towards her.

"Mistress Olivia, I do not wish to use you — only to give. To give you protection, and freedom from the poverty and restriction you know in your brother's house. And passion, such as you have never known —"

She turned sharply away, for his last warmly urgent words brought the flame leaping to her cheeks.

"I do not want it, my lord. I was not made to be a whore. Now will you go?"

"May I not tempt you to walk a little in the garden with me — where all may see us, if that would make you feel safer?"

Olivia shook her head vehemently.

"Leave me alone! I do not want anything you can offer me. I never want to see you again."

He took her chin in his hand, tilting her head back a little so that he could look easily into her face.

"I think you do not know yourself what you really want," he suggested gently. He moved closer, and she thought he would kiss her, and in spite of everything her limbs melted at the thought. But he did not; he only said,

"I will come again tomorrow," and then released her, and before she knew what had happened the door had closed quietly behind him.

Olivia stood trembling violently, swept by an inexplicable depth of emotion. Yet there had been so little in this meeting to trouble her so — one brief touch, no kiss, no caress. And now she felt seared, scorched, as if something behind his quiet manner had reached out to some unknown depth within herself. She buried her face in her hands.

"I must go home!" she whispered aloud. "I must go back to London at once."

Later, when she disclosed her resolution to Celia and Henry, she was greeted with blank dismay.

"But the plague — what of the plague?"

"The deaths have fallen almost every week for a long time now," Olivia returned. "Last week they were under a thousand. I heard that some are already beginning to return to their homes."

"And what of the children? Would you risk the

infection for them?"

So they assumed she would take the children with her! Olivia gave a rueful little smile.

"You did not seem to worry about that before, when the plague was much worse," she pointed out.

"But it is different, choosing to go back."

Olivia wondered if they were most concerned because she was going to escape Lord Alston's importunities; or because they feared that if she went the Westons would see no reason not to turn them out too.

"You can tell your friends that I am making the house ready for your return," she suggested helpfully. "Then if you have more good news of the plague you can come home yourselves. Even the King will not stay in Oxford for ever."

Next day in the chill misty darkness of the early morning Olivia and the children stood yawning beside the London coach. There was still a little time before they were due to depart, and Olivia did not wish them to take their seats until the last possible moment. They would have to sit still for long enough as it was.

Henry had come with them to the inn yard, to see them off, but Olivia had urged him not to wait. It was cold and damp and they had everything they needed. He had been only too glad to make his farewells then and there and return to the warmth and comfort he had left behind him.

Torches set high in sconces on the walls lit the yard with an unsteady, lurid light, flickered over the wet black cobbles, the dark coach, the gleaming flanks of the waiting horses, stamping and snorting in readiness. They also reached out to touch the arched entrance to the yard beyond which four horses pulled a coach at great speed and drew to a shuddering halt. A moment later, a man had leapt from the coach and come running across the yard towards the waiting passengers.

80

"Come!" he said briskly to Olivia. "You will all travel in more comfort with me."

Olivia held the sleeping William closer, and tightened her hold on Barbara's hand.

"My lord! What are you doing here? — and how did you know?"

"From Mistress Warriner, of course. She sent me word last night that you were leaving for London this morning."

Olivia flared into anger.

"When will she learn that I do not need her to manage my affairs — nor you either! Did I not give you my answer yesterday, and all those other times?"

"Ah, but the question is no longer the same." Beneath the lightness of his tone was something new — an unease almost — which startled her into looking at him more intently. But at the same moment he bent suddenly, to crouch down beside Paulina and say pleasantly: "You would like to travel in my coach again, would you not, little maid?"

"Only if Aunt Livvy says so," returned the child gravely. The Earl could not restrain a laugh as he stood up again. "You've taught them well," he told Olivia.

"I wish you would learn as easily," she retorted. "Besides, did you not say that being who I was I could have no further interest for you? You seem to have changed your tune of late — yet I am Olivia Paris still."

She thought, almost, that he coloured, but in the uncertain light she could not be sure.

"Might you not be prepared to change your name — if I could persuade you that it was to your advantage to do so?"

"You must know that I never will. So you waste your time. And if Celia leads you to believe otherwise, she deludes herself, and you — and," she added, glancing about her, "I think you'd better move your

81

coach, or you will cause an obstruction. We are about to leave."

He followed her glance to the increased activity in the yard.

"Damn!" he swore, then turned to her again. "Mistress Olivia, will you not —?"

"No!" she broke in. "Come, children." She turned quickly, starting at a run towards the coach; but he came after her and caught her arm in a grasp so firm in its urgency that she gave a little cry.

"Let me go!" she burst out in sudden fury; but his own words cut across hers, breathless and demanding her instant attention. It was a moment or two before she realised what he had said, and then she could not believe her ears. She stood quite still, staring at him.

"What did you say?"

It was as if he could not now recapture the urgency of before, as if his habitual fluency had deserted him. It seemed a very long time before he spoke again, and when he did so the words were half-drowned by the rumble of the coach as it moved past them over the cobbles towards the archway: unnoticed by either of them. This time, though, she heard what he said, as clearly as if he had shouted.

"I want you to be my wife."

SIX

As if from a great distance Olivia heard Paulina's wail of dismay. "Aunt Livvy, the coach is going!" She felt the small hand tug at hers, but the gesture meant nothing to her. She was aware only of the man facing her, his expression grim as she had never seen it before, daring her to refuse him. Briefly her eyes strayed to where the coach edged narrowly past his own, turned, and disappeared from view. He followed her gaze and said, a little absently yet with a distinct note of triumph,

"You'll have to come with me."

As if roused suddenly from sleep she shook her head vehemently.

"No, never! And as for — that other — I don't think you know what you're saying."

"Then you're wrong. I know exactly what I ask — and what I want. You, and you only — as my wife. Well?"

She remembered the smooth flowery language of his approaches to her in the coach on the way to Spensley, and since, and came close to laughter. But it was not really funny. His tone now was so abrupt that she might have thought he hated her; and what he asked made no possible sense. She could not take him seriously.

"I should have thought the answer to that was quite clear, even to you. We have nothing to offer one another. Now will you leave me alone?" She turned as if to go, but he held her more firmly still.

"You cannot have thought, Mistress Olivia. Consider what it would mean if you were my wife —

Spensley — everything you could wish for —"

"You offered me that once before, and I gave you my answer."

"But that was on other terms. This is quite different."

She turned to look at him, her eyes grave.

"Is it? Can you honestly say that? I know I could not."

"Don't be foolish!" His tone now was sharp with exasperation. "I deserve at least that you should not turn me down outright, here and now. Let me take you to London, then we can talk in peace — while the children sleep —"

Olivia glanced round at the two bright pairs of eyes, full of eager interest, watching them. She smiled faintly.

"Children never sleep when it would be most convenient for them to do so," she pointed out; and then the smile faded and she shook her head again. "But we waste time, my lord. I have no intention of travelling with you."

"Then what will you do? Walk?"

She hesitated a moment and then said with a bravado which hid her very real reluctance. "I shall go back to Mr Weston's house, until tomorrow — or whenever there is a convenient coach."

"Then allow me to see you home, and we can talk at leisure."

"No!" she exclaimed quickly. "Celia and Henry must not know of this — must not even suspect it!" She thought with an inward shudder of their cooing overpowering delight should they hear what Lord Alston offered her. In that, at least, she did not undervalue his proposal. Most women — even those more fortunately placed than she was — would have thought it beyond their wildest dreams.

"Oh," said Lord Alston nonchalantly, "but they know already. I met your brother on my way here,

84

and I have his approval. I am sure he will have told his wife by now."

'So am I,' thought Olivia bitterly. She stood there in the yard, crushed and discouraged. How could she go back now, to face their excitement, and their pleas, the ceaseless pressure to say 'yes' to this man? It would be far harder now to resist them, to find arguments for her own refusal. For a moment she thought it might after all be preferable to set out on foot for London. But she looked at the children, and remembered that other dreadful journey, and knew she could not do that to them. For their sakes at least she must go back. Go back, and hope her old room was still free for her to use, so she could shut herself in there safely beyond the reach of Henry and Celia, until tomorrow. The other alternative — to accept the offer of a ride in Lord Alston's coach — she did not even consider. The thought of enduring several hours of his pleading, with no hope of escape until the journey's end, was unbearable. She raised her head now, and looked at him steadily.

"You are not to come with me," she said with a dignity which concealed her misery. "I have given my answer and I do not wish to see you ever again. Please release my arm."

He did so, but added warningly, "I shall come to see you, when you have had a little time to think. You have not yet given me a fair hearing, and you are not, I think, so unjust as to refuse me that."

Olivia simply pursed her lips and turned away.

"Good day, my lord," she said.

It was as bad as she had expected to find herself ignominiously restored to the company of Henry and Celia and their delighted expectations of a rosy future for her, and for themselves. Her hopes of shutting herself in her room were short-lived. "Oh, it is being cleaned — you cannot go back until tonight," Celia said lightly, when she expressed a wish to rest. "Sit down here by the fire, and we can talk. There is so much to plan —"

"There is nothing to plan," said Olivia firmly, turning to the window, from which she could see the children running free and happy along the garden paths. It was the first time she had said anything herself about Lord Alston's proposal. Until now, Celia had simply chattered without interruption, intoxicated by the golden prospects which awaited them all.

"Nonsense, of course there is — he did not say, of course, where the marriage is to take place, but it is sure to be a splendid affair —"

Olivia closed her eyes wearily.

"Celia," she said, without turning round, "there is to be no marriage. I have no intention of becoming Lord Alston's wife."

The silence then was so long and so complete that Olivia feared some harm had come to her sister-in-law, and turned at last to look at her. But Celia simply stood in frozen dismay, gazing at her with wide-eyed disbelief, with which something approaching horror was clearly mingled.

"You cannot be serious," she said at last.

"Why not? I do not wish to marry him. Isn't that enough?"

"Of course not!" Outrage gave colour to Celia's face. "Olivia, you are poor and friendless and dependent on the charity of others. He is rich and titled and blessed with the favour of the King and court. He is also young and quite deliciously handsome. Maybe he did make dishonourable proposals to you once — but you played your cards very well — even I would never have thought you could manage it quite so well, I must admit — and now he knows he can only have you if he weds you. There's passion for you! You surely can't think of refusing *that*!"

Olivia gave a shudder of disgust at Celia's assessment of the part she had played. Did she really think it had all been a deliberate, calculated scheme on her part? If so, then all the more reason for her to make it very clear that she had no intention of becoming Lady Alston, now or ever.

"I don't want to talk of it," she said firmly. "I shall not marry him, and that's that."

"Olivia, how can you! All your modesty wasted — and what of us? We've cared for you all these years, ungrudgingly, stinting nothing. You can't be so ungrateful as to throw it all in our face, now you have the greatest opportunity any woman could be offered."

"You know I'm grateful to you," said Olivia quietly. "But gratitude is no good reason for marriage."

Celia sniffed. "It's better than many, believe me. And," she added nastily, "do you suppose we shall continue to support you, if you turn down this chance to better yourself, and all of us? I know what Henry will have to say to that."

Olivia could not take the remark very seriously, seeing it simply as a piece of malice on Celia's part, soon over once she knew how certain Olivia was of her own position. But when, later, Henry came in and joined his own pleading to his wife's, she realised that in this at least they were united. Only Henry put it more bluntly still. If she did not accept Lord Alston, he told her, then she would be turned onto the streets and they would have no more to do with her.

'They will change their minds — they must!' she thought to herself. 'Once the first anger is over. They are not cruel people.' But some deeper instinct warned her that there was a limit to their patience, as there had always been. She began as the long morning passed to realise the enormity in their eyes of what she had done by refusing Lord Alston's proposal.

When, early in the afternoon, she heard them

admitting her unwelcome suitor to the house, she felt too discouraged and depressed to care very much. She was closer now to tears than to indignation. She knew only that she must find some way out of this new and horrible dilemma which faced her.

They showed him into the parlour where she sat alone, and closed the door firmly behind him. She knew she need not fear interruption.

She watched him, guardedly, as he stood just inside the door, tall, graceful, assured, and smiling a little. She longed to unsettle his complacency with a withering insult or even a blow; but she had little energy left now, after the battles of the morning. She said only, "You're wasting your time, my lord."

That at least banished the smile from his face, though he came, unperturbed, and took his seat facing her across the hearth.

"I hope not," he said amiably, stretching long brown hands to the blaze. The grimness and uncertainty she had glimpsed in the inn yard seemed to have left him by now, without leaving a trace.

"My answer is no different."

"Why not?" He spoke calmly, as if this was a trivial discussion between friends. "You are alone in the world, and you do not find me unattractive. As my wife you will have a home at Spensley, of which you will, I promise, be sole mistress with all the freedom you could wish for. You will, I hope, have children to care for, in due time. You will want for nothing. You will as far as possible be entirely free to live your own life, without interference."

What was it he had said at Spensley, as he talked to her beneath the portrait of his dead wife? 'She will stay quietly here . . . and never ask to be taken to court . . . or complain. And she will be dutifully blind to the company I keep at my house in London, or at court . . .' The memory chilled her, with its echoes in what he said now.

"And I'll be free to worship as I choose, I suppose?" she said then, her voice deep with irony.

"If you wish," he said equably. "Perhaps I may hope for your eventual conversion – but I shall not expect it, nor press you for it."

She gazed at him sceptically. "What became of the devout obedient little Catholic girl you spoke of not so long ago? You have changed your tune very suddenly."

He shrugged.

"If I have, so what? I do not see you have any cause for complaint in that."

"And will the King smile on your marriage to Olivia Paris? If he would not approve the name in your mistress, I cannot see how he can be expected to like it in a wife."

"Did I not say I hope to persuade you to change your name? What simpler way to do it than this, for you to take mine? I know you would not want a grand court wedding, so we shall be married quietly, and soon, and I will win the King over before I present you to him. I can do so, I assure you."

She stood up suddenly and walked restlessly to the window.

"I don't understand," she said. "Why – why this, all of a sudden? I am no wife for you, surely – nor are you a husband for me, you must see that –"

She heard him cross the room, felt him grasp her shoulders from behind. His hands slid, firm and gentle, down her arms, drawing her near. She felt his mouth on her hair. She felt weak, trembling, ready to sink against him; but she forced herself to stiffen, resisting the seductive appeal of his nearness.

"Would you not like to see your father's portrait hanging again at Spensley?"

She turned then, sharply, her eyes wide with astonishment.

"You would allow *that*! With all you think of him?"

89

He made no move to touch her again, and said, quite seriously, "I don't think I've ever told you what I think of him." She watched him wonderingly as he sat down easily on the window seat nearby and went on "When I first went to Spensley I intended to remove all traces of his occupation from the place. You know, of course, how the regicides are viewed at court — loathed as the most evil of men, guilty of the ultimate sacrilege in taking the life of their anointed King. So I thought too — and still do, to some extent. Yet, it was a strange thing, Olivia. I remember that first night at Spensley coming on your father's portrait, not realising for a moment who he was, thinking only 'what a good face — gentle, kindly, wise'; and the shock of realising my mistake. And there were books he had left, on many subjects, some of which I read to fill an idle moment or two — and I found myself liking what I found there of the man who had owned them and loved them, and whose tolerant spirit reached out to me from their pages. You saw yourself how I kept his collection of pictures, though they too are full of what he was. I do not condone what he did, never think that, and I cannot look on him as anything but the murderer of his King — but I would not, even so, be ashamed that his daughter should hang his portrait in her private chamber; and lie beside me at night, as my honoured wife and the mother of my sons."

For a long time when he had finished speaking his eyes held hers, grave and searching in their expression. She felt moved almost to tears, her anger and bitterness banished by the gentle reflectiveness of his words, by his marked respect for the father she had loved and whom he had never met, except through the possessions he had left behind. For the first time she realised what it would mean to be again at Spensley, knowing it was her home, able to walk in those gardens or sit by the parlour fire, at peace, free from want and from fear of what the future might hold. And if in time there were children, that would only be the better, giving her a purpose, satisfying all her need to love and to be loved. With Celia and Henry, even with their children, she could not hope for that kind of security and that kind of fulfilment. With Lord Alston, as his wife, it could almost be said that she would have everything.

Yet this morning she had rejected him instantly and without hesitation. Surely that first instinct must have been right? For what, after all, could they ever be to one another, so utterly different as they were, the one from the other? It would be like marrying a stranger, simply as a means to regain Spensley and protect herself from hardship.

Yet that after all was what many women did. And this stranger at least was a man with an overwhelming power to attract her, capable as she knew of real kindness, when he chose. Could she ask for any more? If she refused him now she faced destitution and rejection and a life of unknown, unimaginable hardship. If she accepted, she would go back to the home she loved, to live there in peace and security, close again to her beloved father whose essential goodness had reached even beyond the grave to touch the man who wanted now, for reasons it was perhaps better not to consider, to make her his wife. She bent her head, gazing down at her hands, tight clasped before her.

"Yes," she whispered. "Yes, I'll marry you."

After that, it was as if she no longer had any control at all over events, as if she were simply whirled along by the whims and wishes of those around her. She was never alone. At the same time she saw little of Lord Alston, except as a distant figure deep in conversation with Henry, or hurrying in to discuss some plan or other with Celia, and with scarcely time for the briefest of words with herself. It seemed that now the marriage was arranged, she had no further part to play, except as a trivial pawn in the elaborate game taking place around her. Even when Celia and the seamstress bullied her into standing for long tedious hours while they chatted and pinned and cut and stitched, she might have been an inanimate dummy for all the notice they took of her.

"Yes," Celia would say, standing back with her head on one side, running critical eyes over the folds of creamy silk, "yes, it looks well enough — but should not the bodice be taken in further? And the skirt does not hang right there, can you see?" There would be a vigorous tugging at the already close-fitting bodice, a rearranging of the shining folds of the skirt, a twitch at the full, slashed sleeves, and Celia would nod her approval, or make a further suggestion. No one ever asked Olivia what she thought; and in truth she did not really care. It all seemed very remote and unreal, and she could not believe that any of it had anything much to do with her.

And then, on the night before the appointed wedding day, one week after she had so impulsively given her consent, she had a little time alone at last. She was not, even then, completely alone, but the children with whom she shared her room were deeply asleep, and she stood at the open window, oblivious of the bitter air reaching her from the shadowy garden, staring into the darkness and realising with force, for the first time, that tomorrow she would take a momentous and irrevocable step.

'What have I done?' she thought with sudden panic. She could have said 'no' to that astounding proposal; she could somehow have faced her brother's fury. In London there were friends who shared her religious faith who would, she was sure, have made certain she did not starve. It would not have been easy; but it would have been possible.

Yet here she was, about to marry a man whom she

could neither respect nor like, with whom she had nothing in common, however much he might arouse the passion she despised. And for what? For the sake of Spensley, and the memories it held for her. Yet when, tomorrow, she found herself again at Spensley, would she be able to face those memories? Would her father's spirit ask her how she could bring herself to marry such a man, for such a slight reward? Would Luke's presence, haunting the quiet garden, demand to know how she could have sold herself for such a mockery of a marriage?

That it would be a mockery, she saw very clearly now. Lord Alston had desired her with all the passion of a young and healthy man faced with an attractive woman who had spurned him. He had found that nothing would induce her to become his mistress. And so, throwing common sense and worldly advantage to the winds, he had offered her marriage, as the only way to make her his own. But she saw now, only too well, that his interest in her would be no more permanent than if she had become his mistress. Once he tired of her — as inevitably he would, for human passion without friendship or affection to sustain it was a short-lived thing — then he would leave her to go in search of other entertainment: a mistress at his London house, perhaps, or a pretty actress. The vows he would make tomorrow were simply a means of securing Olivia for his bed, for as long as he should find her attractive. Once that was over they would mean nothing to him. True, as his mistress she would have had no security for her old age, or for her children; as his wife she might well look forward to living in comfort at Spensley until the end of her days. But tonight, with sudden insight, Olivia saw that she had behaved exactly as Celia had so admiringly accused her of doing, by using her power to attract for her own cynical ends. She had not set out to do so, knowingly and with open eyes;

but the result was the same. Staring into the night, she did not like the Olivia Paris whom she saw there, and she shuddered at what she had done.

Perhaps, she thought — perhaps I should turn back now, tell them all I cannot, and must not, go through with it. That would, after all, be the only honourable course to take, before it was too late. So, she was sure, her father, or Luke her dear friend, would have advised her.

She had closed the window and was on the point of going at once to tell Celia and Henry of her decision, when William woke from a nightmare and had to be comforted; and when at last he was asleep again she was too tired to do anything but tumble into bed, her resolution gone, almost forgotten now. It did not seem to matter any more. The clarity of thought which had come to her at the window seemed to have left her. Time enough tomorrow to decide what to do, if anything.

The next day the whirl of activity seized her again, from the moment she awoke finally from a restless sleep. There was no time to think, or to question the impulsive decision she had made. The marriage was to take place in the morning, at the Westons' house — whatever they might think of his morals, they were flattered that so great a man as Lord Alston should choose to be married beneath their roof. A Catholic priest — at the Earl's express request — would come, discreetly, to conduct the ceremony, and only close friends and family would be allowed into the secret and invited to be present. Afterwards, there would be the briefest of festivities before he took his new Countess at once to Spensley for their wedding night.

The time passed that morning with terrifying swiftness. Afterwards, Olivia could remember very little of it, until the moment when she stood in the parlour, a slender silent bride in the creamy silk which showed off her slight figure to perfection; her glossy hair falling loose about her, except where pearls threaded its shining darkness. And there, standing now at her side, was the man she was to marry, to her surprise as gravely unsmiling as she, for all the splendour of cinnamon satin and sapphire ribbon knots which clothed his magnificent figure. Facing them, black clad and austere, was the small neat man who was the first Catholic priest Olivia had ever seen. He did not look a dangerous and subversive figure, and when he began the service, in a quiet clear voice, there was nothing unduly disturbing in that either: Olivia had been well-taught in Latin, so that the meaning of the prayers was not lost on her.

They came at last to the vows, the words as simple and solemn as if she were any carefree country girl come to church to wed the sweetheart of her choice. Now she, Olivia, promised to take Benedict as her husband, through all the chances life might bring; as Benedict in his turn had vowed to care for her with equal fidelity. She felt his hand close about hers, warm, oddly protective in its gentle strength. And she thought: 'This will not be a mockery. I shall try with all my power to keep the vow I make today. I shall be a good wife to him, and seek to win his love in return. Perhaps, in time, we shall grow together, and find real companionship.'

As he took her hand to slip his ring onto her finger, she raised her eyes to his, and thought perhaps, for a moment, that she read the same resolve in them.

Later, when he kissed her, she felt her body leap to life in answer to his momentary fervour, and thought with a trembling excitement of the coming night. What would it be like, that moment when she was free at last to surrender herself to him?

But first there were the festivities to endure, and for all Lord Alston's demands, Celia and Henry had made them as elaborate as their resources would allow. Olivia had never seen such an abundant variety of food on display as faced her today; and she was sure that many of the guests present in the crowded rooms were neither close friends nor family. But perhaps they were the Earl's guests, after all.

There was a consort of viols playing with vigour in a corner of the hall, and once the eating was over the dancing began. Olivia, who had sat silently at the table, scarcely eating, and not looking at all at the Earl seated beside her, as silent as she, felt him touch her arm.

"We must dance once, to please them," he said softly. "Then we can go."

She felt him take her hand, and allowed him to lead her onto the floor, uncomfortably conscious of the many watching eyes, and of her own inadequate skill in dancing.

"You dance quite well," he said in an undertone, after a moment or two. There was such a note of surprise in his voice that she laughed a little, in spite of herself.

"My father was not averse to every kind of pleasure," she told him. "I had lessons as a child, like most young girls."

"Ah, your brother led me to believe you had your head stuffed full of mathematics, and not much else. You are clearly more accomplished than he gave you credit for."

"Thank you," she said lightly, wondering what else Henry had said, and what he had been asked; and then the movement of the dance drew them apart. When they met again he acknowledged her only with a grave and unreadable glance of his blue eyes that told her nothing.

There was laughter and much coarse joking and shouting as the guests saw the Earl and his bride into the coach that was to take them to Spensley. Olivia endured it as best she could, with a stiff little smile and a sense of relief that they would not have to endure the noisy and public bedding customary on such occasions. When one was much in love with one's bridegroom then perhaps it would be bearable. But in these present circumstances — she could only be thankful that they would be facing the start of their new life together without an audience.

When the coach drew slowly away leaving the shouts and the laughter behind, Olivia pulled the folds of her new furred cloak about her, and drew the hood forward to shade her face, and closed her eyes. She felt suddenly very tired, as if the events of the day had drawn far more strength from her than she had realised at the time. She wished very much indeed that she could be alone.

She wondered after a time if her companion was similarly exhausted, for he too sat completely still, saying nothing. She stole a glance at him from the corner of her eyes, and saw that he, like her just now, had his eyes closed. In a moment, though, aware of her gaze, he opened them and smiled suddenly.

"My Olivia," was all he said, in a whisper. And then he reached across the space which separated them and took her hand in his. She could feel him trembling, for all the strength of his clasp. Yet now that she was free to yield herself to whatever passion he woke in her, she felt nothing, no answering excitement, no stir of desire. Panic-stricken, she thought: 'Will we not even have that now, to bring us together?' Her eyes, wide and frightened, searched his face for some kind of reassurance, some hope for their future.

As if in response, he slid his arm about her and drew her close, holding her so that her head rested on his shoulder. Then he sat quite still, until the exhausted tension eased from her body, and she felt only safe, and warm, and drowsy. After a while she even fell asleep.

97

She woke with a start to a moment of dazed confusion before she remembered where she was and how she had come to be there. The coach had stopped, and her companion — her bridegroom — was shaking her gently and saying, "Come, Olivia, we are home."

Feeling a little dizzy and stupid with sleep, she waited as he stepped down from the coach, and then allowed him to help her down. The sharp air of the bright November day cleared her head a little.

On the drive before the main door of Spensley — her home again — the servants stood in line to welcome them. Olivia walked along, guided by the Earl's hand on her arm, acknowledging each respectful greeting with an automatic smile, which she hoped would look warm and friendly to its recipient. She felt too stiff and uncomfortable to manage anything more.

She found herself at last before the familiar figure of Tom, the gardener, and felt him take both hands in his warm clasp, and say in a fervent undertone, "Welcome home, Mistress Olivia — I'm that glad — you'll be the making of him, that you will." She saw that there were tears in his eyes, and this time her smile had in it all the affection he could have desired.

Inside, the Earl ordered supper to be brought to them in their room. "We'll be warm there by the fire," he told Olivia. And then he led her, without haste, up the wide stairs to the great bedchamber in which, once, her parents had slept.

The bed was new, though, elaborately carved and bright with richly-embroidered hangings; and so was the Turkish carpet on the polished floor; and the upholstered chairs by the table before the great hearth. Her father would never have allowed so lavish a fire, either, in what was merely a room in which to sleep.

But of course today it was not only for sleeping. Olivia remembered that as she stood in the doorway, looking round; and shivered involuntarily. Dimly she was aware of the Earl closing the door behind them, and then coming to lift the cloak from her shoulders and lead her to the chair which stood nearest to the fire. He stood back then, waiting, watching her without a word, until the servants had laid the supper on the table and left. Olivia sat very still, looking down at her clasped hands. Her heart was beating fiercely, and she knew fear was uppermost in her at this moment: not physical fear, but fear for the future, fear of the step she had taken today and from which she could not now turn away.

She heard wine being poured into a glass, and knew the Earl was handing it to her. She took it, without meeting his eyes, murmuring her thanks. It was warm and spicy, and she sipped thankfully, feeling life return to numbed limbs, some small courage to her shrinking spirit.

"Will you eat?" he asked quietly after a moment, and she shook her head, still not looking at him. She heard him pour wine for himself, and heard, briefly, the clatter of a plate. Evidently he was able to eat, if she was not.

There was silence again, a long silence broken only by the hiss and crackle of burning wood in the hearth, the distant sound of an owl, far off in the trees beyond the curtained windows. Olivia's glass was empty and she stared at it, turning it idly in her hands; and then, eventually, reached over and laid it on the table. As she withdrew her hand, his own closed about it, the long fingers moving caressingly over her wrist.

"Olivia — come —" The whispered words seemed to quiver through her, setting up a vibration compounded of apprehension and something close to the desire which she had feared had left her for ever. She raised her eyes at last to look at him, and the blue of his answering glance, darkened with passion, struck a flame deep inside her, driving out all the fear and confusion and weariness of the day, leaving only a desperate hunger in its place, a hunger which now at last could be satisfied.

He slid to his knees and took both her hands in his and drew her down to face him before the leaping fire. Those great roaring flames were nothing to the ones which burned in her now, as his hands with speed and tenderness unlaced her gown and drew it from her and laid her naked beneath their caressing touch. She ran her own hands eagerly under his doublet, feeling the lines of his strong body through the silk shirt, drawing him nearer, nearer, until finally they lay together in a delight and ecstasy beyond her wildest imaginings, fused as one body in the glow of the fire; and all her longings were laid to rest at last.

SEVEN

It seemed as if the intoxicating sweetness of their first night together, the long lovely hours during which they slept at all only to wake and turn again to the other's embrace, had set a seal on their marriage with its promise of real and lasting happiness.

Olivia would never forget how, when the fire died low and even the lingering warmth of their first love-making was no longer enough to keep out the cold, he had carried her to the bed and there between the silken sheets made love to her once more; and then they had slept a little, she cradled in his arms, her head on his chest. And so the night had passed, with few words between them, for there was no need for words.

The glow of ecstasy lingered with Olivia through the day that followed, filling her with a certainty that after all everything would be well; that she had not made a terrible mistake. Yet afterwards she realised, looking back, that if it had not been for those nights of mutual delight, then she would have felt very differently about her new state.

Even as it was, the daylight and the need to eat, and talk, and walk about observed by servants, brought an immediate awkwardness between them. It was then that Olivia realised that she scarcely knew this man who had possessed her with such wild passion. He was almost a stranger, though she was fast becoming acquainted with every taut line of his lean and powerful body. As they faced each other across the table set with a tempting breakfast, Olivia felt all at once oddly shy. How, she wondered, was a new bride supposed to behave on this first day? What would her duties be in this place she had known so well, and yet under such very different circumstances? How would her husband expect her to talk, and address the servants, and conduct herself in public towards himself? Would he be angry if she failed to satisfy him?

She searched rather anxiously for some topic of conversation which might bring them closer together, some shared interest they could talk about, to bring them as near in mind as they had been through the night in body. But she realised that she had almost no idea what his interests were, and none at all as to what he would regard as a suitable subject for talk at breakfast time. They ate in a silence which Olivia would have found uncomfortable had her body not been so filled with contentment, their eyes meeting shyly from time to time, and then quickly looking away again.

Afterwards he took her to meet the housekeeper, and left her there to be shown the kitchens and dairies and storerooms, the linen press and the rooms where the servants slept, and everything else which might be supposed to concern her as the new mistress of Spensley. It was a strange sensation, seeing the changes which had come about since she lived here as a girl, feeling only half at home because she was no longer a child at ease under her father's roof. She had not thought it would be quite like this. It would take time even to get to know Spensley as well as once she had done.

She met her new husband again at dinner, a meal only a little less silent than breakfast had been. The Earl made an effort to engage her in conversation. He talked of the weather, and touched on the news from court, and described a new and fashionable song with real enthusiasm; and he was unfailingly polite and kind. But he was nevertheless a stranger, a man unknown to her and for the moment unknowable. She had felt closer to him before they married, when he had talked so warmly of her father. She knew that it was that one moment of sympathy which had made her accept his proposal of marriage; yet now they seemed so far removed from it that it was hard to believe it had ever happened. She was tempted to say something about her father, in the hope that they might after all recapture some kind of brief intimacy; but she felt too shy and awkward to speak of anything so near to her heart, for to fail would be worse than if she had never tried.

After dinner, they walked in the garden, pausing to talk to Tom as he worked, and discussing various ideas for alterations and developments. For that little time at least they forgot their constraints, talking easily and happily and with laughter, and finding that they were almost completely in agreement. Olivia found it hard to believe that her husband had an enthusiasm for gardens, but if it was simply courtesy and consideration for her which moved him this afternoon, then it was very successful in setting her, almost, at her ease. It was only when they went in to supper that the strangeness returned. But afterwards, when he sang to her, the music he chose held all the promise of the night to come, and by the time he came to lead her to bed her shyness had gone.

That first night and day set the pattern for the early weeks of their marriage. At night, together in bed, passion united them in a darkness shot through with flames of delight. By day, though there were moments of something approaching closeness, they were for the most part courteous strangers, living side by side and yet always separate. For all that, Olivia began to hope that in time she would come to know the man beneath the polished surface, and to find there a friend and a companion. She had to acknowledge though that it was a great deal to hope for, and far more than she had once thought possible. Then, she had expected only to find a lover, at best; and that at least she had. She wondered why it should matter so much now that he should be more. And she tried not to allow herself to fear that she might find in the end that, as she had once believed, she had nothing in common with him.

They had been at Spensley for two weeks when they received their first visitor. They were at dinner in the parlour when he came, discussing their plans for the garden: it was therefore a happier meal than many they had shared. Olivia felt a pang of disappointment when the sound of a horse on the drive outside broke into their talk.

The Earl paused in mid-sentence, rose to his feet and went to the window. Olivia heard him give an exclamation; then he said hastily, "Excuse me a moment — I shall not be long," and he left the room.

Olivia continued to eat, aware that her husband was greeting the new arrival: she heard their voices outside though she could not hear what was said. Then they must have come indoors, for she heard nothing more. She expected that at any moment they would come into the room, and she braced herself to play the part of the welcoming hostess, a little nervous in case she should not do it well.

But they did not come. In the end, tired of waiting and curious as to what should be keeping them so long, she left the table and went to investigate.

They were not far away. As she opened the door leading into the hall she heard voices just beyond it. The newcomer must have been speaking, for she did not recognise the faintly languid tones.

"— *That* will hardly help your reputation, my dear Benedict," he was saying. Olivia stood still, listening, wondering whether she ought after all to interrupt or simply to go away again. "The King is not pleased," he went on. The words could not have alarmed her husband very much, for she knew from his tone in reply that he was smiling.

"He will get over that in time. He is never angry for long. As for my reputation, surely a Puritan wife is exactly what I need to set any suspicions at rest. Don't you agree?"

So they were talking of her! Olivia felt her heart beat faster, and wondered what else had been said, and what would come next. And why did he think marriage to her should be good for his reputation? That seemed a very odd remark, set against the news of the King's displeasure.

'They say eavesdroppers hear no good of themselves,' she thought ruefully; and decided she did not want to hear any more. Sometimes it was more comfortable to be kept in ignorance. She did not want anything to spoil the delicate bloom of her new happiness, and her hopes for its growth. Resolutely she pushed the door fully open as noisily as she was able; and the two men turned to look at her.

"You seemed to be gone a long time," she said, with a note of apology.

The Earl did not appear to be in the least perturbed by the interruption, but simply smiled and came towards her.

"Olivia, you must meet my oldest friend, James Fontwell. He attended our wedding, but I think you may not remember him — and he must make your closer acquaintance now too."

She did remember him, slightly, but only to know that she had seen the plump brown-haired man with his languidly indolent manner somewhere in the crowd on that strange confused day. Now, she was aware of his appraising glance as she approached him, and the spark of approval as he took in her graceful figure in the simple crimson gown, the shining hair knotted with ribbons, the delicacy of her complexion, warmed to glowing colour by her new experience of physical delight. He took her hand and bent to kiss it, his eyes lingering all the while on her face.

"I too could have risked disfavour for such a treasure," he murmured in a tone which brought added colour to Olivia's face. She thought, glancing at her husband, that he did not look entirely pleased at the compliment.

However, the next moment he had invited their guest to join them for dinner, and Olivia, anxious to show how dutiful a wife she was, set herself to amuse and entertain her husband's oldest friend. There was no depth to their talk, but she found it surprisingly easy to make him laugh, and to turn his sometimes too-lavish compliments with a light witticism which only made him think more kindly of her still. She suspected that she would not approve of his style of life were she to find out much about it, but she liked him and found him pleasant company. She tried not to wonder what escapades and adventures he might have shared with her husband.

To her surprise she realised after a time that the Earl had ceased to take any part at all in the conversation. Instead, he had sunk into a gloomy silence from which he would not even emerge to join in his friend's laughter. Olivia watched him, wondering with alarm what she had done to offend him. In the end it was a relief when the meal ended and the Earl took his friend's arm and said to her, with unaccustomed curtness: "We have business to discuss. You must amuse yourself this afternoon."

It was bitterly cold and raining hard, so Olivia did not walk in the garden as she had hoped to do. Instead she went upstairs to the pretty room which had been set aside for her own private use. She had been greatly touched to find it ready for her when she came to Spensley, for once it had been her own bedroom. She supposed that the Earl had somehow discovered that fact — from Tom perhaps — and decided that there her parents' portraits should be hung, and there a writing desk and chairs, a table and chest and carved bookcase should be placed ready for her enjoyment and her use. It was the one place where she could relax and feel truly at home.

She went now to the window, its low wide sill cushioned in a pale green velvet which echoed the colour of the painted walls, and looked out at the drenched and leafless garden. She felt deeply uneasy, as if today's visit, so harmless and pleasurable on the surface, had not only broken into their solitude but also in some way threatened the happiness they had. Yet she could not say why, except that Benedict was displeased in some way. Perhaps after all he had not liked her interruption, in which case she must somehow make her peace with him. She wished though she could shake off the gloom which had settled all at once over her spirits.

When the Earl came to take her to supper he was frowning still, and she rose quickly to her feet in alarm, letting her book slide to the floor.

"Is your friend staying to supper?" she asked, trying to calm herself.

"No," said the Earl curtly. "He has gone."

She retrieved the book, and laid it carefully on the window seat, and then looked at her husband.

"What have I done to displease you?" she asked gravely.

"Nothing at all," he said in surprise. "I am not displeased." He spoke with such a note of severity that she could not believe him; but he left her no possibility of pursuing the matter.

She came and laid her hand on the arm he held out to her, and tried to introduce a lighter note by saying: "I liked your friend."

"So I observed." His voice was sharp with irony, and the tone caused her to shoot a quick glance at his face. Was that what was wrong? Had he thought her behaviour too familiar towards his friend? Could he even – strange thought – be jealous? She pressed his arm with her fingers and said softly: "But I'm glad we're alone again. It's better that way." And though he said nothing she knew that his mood lightened. He did not talk very much at supper time, but the displeasure had gone.

It was at the very end of supper, as she told herself she had been foolish to be afraid, that he shattered all her restored peace of mind.

"Tomorrow I go to court," he said abruptly.

"Tomorrow! But why? You said nothing before."

"I told you often enough that you would be asked to remain quietly here while I was at court – and I think I made it plain that would happen often. I have duties there. And did I not say I would have to win the King's approval for our marriage? It is time I was back in Oxford. I've been away too long."

There was nothing to say. He could not tell her how long he would be away. He might, he said, even find it necessary to be absent for Christmas; but he knew she was not used to lavish celebrations of the season and would not mind. Olivia remembered her father's disapproval of what he regarded as a pagan festival, and knew she ought not to mind, but found even so that she did. Only, she could do nothing but accept what he said with a good grace, and wish that the night that followed need never end.

It did end, of course; and in the cold grey dawn he stood by the waiting coach to draw her into a last lingering embrace and whisper, "I'll be back when I can, sweet – think of me when you lie in bed." And then he was gone.

She stood gazing along the empty drive long after the coach had disappeared from view until it grew too cold to stay there any longer. The day seemed interminable. She discussed the meals with the housekeeper, and supervised the servants, and read a little, and sewed, and realised after what seemed like hours that it was still only early afternoon, and yet there seemed to be nothing left to do. After some aimless wandering from room to room — each one seeming more empty than the last — she put on her furred cloak and went into the garden.

That, too, seemed more desolate than usual, grey and devoid of growth and colour: the spring was still a long way off. Today there was not even Tom for company: his wife was sick, and he had been given the day off to be with her. 'Perhaps later,' thought Olivia, 'I'll go and see them.'

She wandered forlornly through the rose garden where a chill little wind rattled the few shrivelled leaves, and on into the formal Italian garden beyond, all dark low hedges, grey statues and narrow paths. At the far end, beyond a frozen pool and motionless fountain, stood a low stone seat. She glanced towards it — and then stood quite still with shock. For it was occupied, by a gaunt dark figure whom she did not know.

Almost at once he saw her and rose to his feet, and she pressed her hand to her mouth and wondered whether to run. And then he moved towards her and something in the way he walked struck her to the heart with its total familiarity. She gave a little cry of wondering astonishment. Could it be —? Here, where he had so often walked with her, years ago —?

She dared not trust her eyes. She waited with fast-beating heart, watching intently as he came nearer.

He was older of course, as she was: very thin, haggard almost, his dark hair unkempt, his face unshaven, hollow with hunger or sickness about the eyes and beneath the prominent cheekbones. His clothes were worn, the sober patched garments of a Puritan gentleman fallen on hard times. And then all at once he smiled and she no longer had any doubts at all. With a cry of gladness she ran to his embrace and

109

clung to him, laughing and crying at one and the same moment.

"Luke! Oh Luke, after all this time!"

He held her close, one hand caressing her hair, and she could feel an emotion as deep as hers vibrating through his body. She heard him murmur her name in the quiet warm voice she remembered so well. It was as if she had heard it last only yesterday.

Much later she drew away from him a little, and studied him with affectionate concern.

"What are you doing here? How did you come? Why are you in England at all? — And you look so ill — Oh, but Luke it is so *good* to see you!"

He smiled, but only for an instant, and then he said in a quiet tone from which all warmth had gone:

"I came back to marry you. I thought we could go to America together."

She could think of nothing to say. She was aware of a tearing pain deep inside, and a desperate sense of bitter irony. If only he had come a month ago, two weeks even — her friend and companion, her beloved Luke who had grown up at her side and understood and shared her every thought and mood! And now it was too late. She had been wrong after all to go on with this marriage, so practical and reasonable though it had seemed in worldly terms. If only she had known!

She bent her head, struggling to bring herself under control. She knew that a very little would make her weep. When she did speak at last it was huskily, and with great difficulty, though what she said was unemotional enough.

"You must have had a difficult crossing at this time of year." It sounded pointless, but she had to say something to cover her distress.

"I landed in England at the end of August," he said.

She flung her head back, her breath drawn sharply in.

"August! Then why did you not come before?"
This time the anguish in her voice was unmistakable.
He must have heard it, for his hands tightened about
her elbows, steadying her.

"I could not. I have been in prison."

That, then, explained his gaunt appearance. She
gave a little cry.

"Why? What happened?"

He smiled ruefully, and shrugged.

"Little enough. I sought out some old friends when
I reached London — by then you had left, I suppose
because of the plague. It seemed I chose the wrong
company. They had been embroiled in some hot-
headed and ill-conceived plot to take the Tower, and
as I was with them —" He shrugged again. "They
have only now let me go." He paused, and then went
on: "I went at once to find you, and there heard —
Why, Olivia? Why did you marry him? I could not
believe it." She saw his glance run over her, resting
for a moment on her trim waist glimpsed through the
folds of her cloak. "Did he get you with child?" he
asked very gently.

She felt the colour flood her face.

"No; no, it was not that."

"It must be a love match then, I suppose," he
commented gloomily. "But for such a man! I would
not have thought it of you, Olivia."

She shook her head.

"No," she said quietly. "I don't love him. But —"
What could she say? 'I married him so I could come
back to Spensley?' It sounded very trivial as a reason
for marriage. Yet she must somehow make Luke
understand. "I was very alone, Luke — and not very
happy. It seemed a way out — to have my own
establishment, here, where I was at home —"

"That doesn't sound like you, Olivia — to sell yourself like any whore for worldly advantage."

She coloured fierily and exclaimed at his indignant

111

tone. Yet what he said only echoed what she herself had thought on the night before her marriage.

"He has been very kind —" she faltered.

"'Has been'? Then you are not certain he will continue to be? That shows what you really think of him. From what I hear he is not and never could be the man for you."

"You don't know him," she said defensively; and thought: 'Do I?' After all, she had seen so many sides of Benedict Alston: the smooth courtier, setting out to seduce her, cynical and worldly; the man who thought well of her father; the husband who could be jealous when she showed friendliness to their guest; the passer-by who gave shelter to a sick child; the man who drowned his fear of death in drink; the passionate lover; the kindly stranger; the man who this morning had left her abruptly and almost without warning to return to the court from which she was excluded — Were these all part of the same man, or was there someone else, someone whom as yet she scarcely guessed at? It was hard to defend her marriage to Luke when she was so unsure of her own feelings.

Perhaps Luke realised how his questioning disturbed her, for he conceded at last; "No, I don't know him — and I don't mean to hurt you by speaking ill of him. Only, it was bad enough to find you married — and when I found it was to *him* —" He broke off, and gazed at her earnestly. "Olivia, if ever you need me — if he ill-uses you in any way —"

"He won't — I'm sure he won't." She spoke confidently, but even as she did so she thought; 'I can't even be sure of that — not really sure.' Trying desperately to change the subject, she went on: "But aren't you going back to America soon?"

Luke frowned. "I don't know, Olivia. Now that I know things are — as they are — And there is something else, something important, that I have to do

112

first. It may be that I shall never go back."

It was easier to talk of his plans, safely clear of the dangerous submerged rocks of her marriage, and his feelings for her, which could so easily wreck all her peace of mind. As they talked they began to walk back towards the stone seat and sat there, hands linked, two friends completely at ease in one another's company.

"What kind of thing is it?" Olivia asked. "Not more trouble, I hope?"

"You know I'm no hothead — but I do have ideals, as you have, for which I care deeply. And I suppose this is still my country — I was born and bred here — and if I see that some danger threatens our peace and freedom it is up to me to play my part in repelling that danger."

"Luke — you *are* in trouble! Is that not so? Or you will be, if you're not careful."

"I shall be careful, but there are things I must do whatever the risk. It's better though that you know nothing about it — especially now."

"Why not? I'm not a different person simply because I'm married. You know I'm your loyal friend, and always will be. Don't you trust me?"

"Of course — but it is your safety I fear for, a little." He paused for a moment, and then continued earnestly: "Has it not occurred to you to wonder why a man like Lord Alston should *want* to marry you? Oh, you're beautiful and virtuous and so on, I know, but that alone would not be enough, would it? Especially considering who your father was."

The question so exactly echoed what she had asked herself from time to time that she felt uneasy. Yet she thought she had answered it to her own satisfaction. Her own answer though was not one that she cared to give to Luke.

"Wouldn't it?" she returned feebly. "What is your explanation then?"

"I don't want to tell you everything — but perhaps it would be better if you were put on your guard — I think, from what I know, and my friends have discovered, that he would find it to his advantage to have a wife of such very Puritan stock."

"I shouldn't have thought so — the King is displeased, I understand." But what was it she had heard him say last night? 'A Puritan wife is exactly what I need to set any suspicions at rest'. Remembering that, she dared not meet Luke's gaze in case he read her uneasiness there.

"That is on the surface — and the King may or may not be a part of the scheme. We know so little yet — but we are sure that Lord Alston has at least some part in it, if only a small one. I mustn't tell you any more — but be on your guard — and remember that I am always your friend, should you need one."

"Then you must tell me what all this is about! You can't just leave it at dark hints and warnings. That is more frightening than knowing everything."

"*I* don't know everything. If I did there would be nothing left to do. But remember that Lord Alston is a Papist, that the King is said to have Papist sympathies, and his Queen and half his courtiers are Papists — and that the avowed aim of every Papist is to win England back for the Pope. There you will find part of the answer to your questions."

Olivia's eyes widened. She thought of Lord Alston, the worldly courtier interested only in women and his own comfort. For all her doubts about him, she could not believe that beneath his frivolous exterior lay a bigot plotting to further a religion for which he showed little more than the slightest of enthusiasm.

On the other hand he had insisted that a Catholic priest marry them, even though that was, strictly speaking, forbidden by law: perhaps after all his religion meant more to him than appearances suggested.

114

"You see, Olivia, there have been contacts with the French on just that matter — we *know* that — only we don't know the details, or who is involved, or how or why. We only have our suspicions. All I am sure of is that it must be stopped."

"But how can you be sure if you don't even know what 'it' is?"

"We know enough — Would you be prepared to see French troops brought in to force us all to turn Catholic — with all the imprisonings and burnings and cruelty that it would mean — and no freedom for any of us to worship as we choose?"

"We haven't much freedom as it is."

"I know — but this would be worse. You cannot deny that, surely?"

"No, of course I cannot. But you may be wrong."

"We may be — I hope so indeed — but I don't think so. And I have told you more than I meant to. You will have to be very careful — it would be better if the connection between us were not known."

"But then I shan't be able to see you!"

"You will — I shall come quietly like this when your husband is away."

Olivia frowned.

"I don't think I like that — it seems disloyal —"

"Disloyal! When your husband is using you for his own ends? Oh, Olivia!"

"You don't know that — and I made a solemn vow —"

"Where? Before whom? I don't suppose it was a godly minister who married you."

"No," Olivia admitted uncomfortably. "It was a Catholic priest."

"There you are then! It's probably not even legal."

"But I meant the vow when I made it — and I must be true to him unless he makes it impossible for me to be so — Please, Luke, believe me when I say that —"

115

He patted her hand gently.

"I do, Olivia — and I understand. I'll let it rest there. Just take care, and remember you have a friend."

She smiled at him, a little wanly; and changed the subject.

"What became of you in America? You've told me nothing of that."

He was silent for a short while, and then he said: "It seems so long ago now, and so far away — as it is, I suppose. It was hard at first, very hard. And I found there was as much intolerance in Massachusetts as there was here, if of a different kind. But in the end I found a settlement of men and women who thought as I did, and a couple, husband and wife, who gave me work on their farm. They had no children, and they are growing old, and I became very fond of them, and they of me — it was as if we were one family. They made it clear that I was to be like a son to them, and the farm would be mine afterwards. I told them about you, and we planned how you would come to live there with us — I think we could have been happy —" He broke off abruptly, and she saw that the pain he felt was as deep as her own. So that was what she had turned her back on when she sold herself for Spensley! She could have grown to love that distant farm as deeply as she loved this place, she knew that. She would have found a home there, ready made: the kindly old people; Luke at her side; his children growing around her. It was, now, an unbearable vision. She gave a little choking cry and turned to cling to him, weeping for all that might have been. And Luke held her and caressed her and tried to comfort her for a loss which he felt as deeply as did she.

They did not see the tall figure approaching them along the path in the fading daylight. They knew nothing until he stood looking down at them and his voice vibrating with anger broke in on their

116

anguish.

"So *that's* how you pass your time when I'm away! It hasn't taken you long to find consolation, wife!"

They sprang apart. Olivia felt as if a blow had struck all the breath from her body and the blood from her veins. She was white and trembling. Yet for a moment, looking up at the tall golden figure gazing at her with eyes blazing with a fury such as she had never seen before she had the odd sensation that he was not quite real. He was a figure from a dream — a dream now turned nightmare; and it was Luke, her old friend at her side who was real, who was a part of her. If only she had realised that in time, and known that it was with him, and all that was known and beloved, that she belonged.

Shakily, smoothing her skirts and her hair, she rose to her feet.

"You're wrong," she said unsteadily. "It's not what you think."

He grasped her arm, and she could feel the anger quivering through him.

"Isn't it? What is it then? Tell me that!"

"We — we are old friends — I knew Luke long ago, when we were children. He has been away, and only came back today."

"Choosing his time with care, I note — or did you send him word the moment I left the house?"

"No! Of course not! — Please, believe me, there is nothing —"

Luke moved forward, as if ready to protect Olivia yet afraid that a wrong move on his part might goad the Earl to violence.

"My lord, your wife is blameless, I can assure you. What she says is quite true. We are like brother and sister, that's all."

'But we could have been more,' thought Olivia, even as she willed her husband to believe what Luke

117

said. Perhaps he read some of what she thought in her eyes, for he only returned furiously: "Get into the house, wife — and, you, go at once — I never want to see you again, here or anywhere!"

There was no point in arguing further. Olivia turned and made her way, weeping painfully, back towards the house which no longer seemed to offer a shelter and a haven, for in choosing it as her prize she had lost a greater one. And Luke, after a moment, swung on his heel and walked grimly away. The Earl waited until he had disappeared through the wicket gate leading into the woods, and then set out at a brisk pace after his wife.

EIGHT

Olivia went at once without pausing to her own room and sank down on the window seat; and there very soon the Earl found her.

He closed the door behind him and stood watching her with a grim quietness which was more frightening than his rage had been.

"Well?" he said at last. "What have you to say now?"

"Nothing," she replied, fighting to control her tears. "It is all quite true. I have not deceived you, and never would." 'But have *you* deceived me?' she wondered, against her will. Was Luke right in what he had hinted?

"Then why did you meet him there like that? Why did he not come to the door openly, like any other guest? Tell me that, pray?"

"How did you know he didn't?" asked Olivia defiantly, playing for time.

"Because the servants knew nothing about him, of course. I was told you were walking alone in the garden. I imagined you sad, and lonely — missing me, perhaps. So I came quickly to comfort you — and that's what I found, you in passionate embrace with a stranger — and you expect me to believe your talk of long-lost friends and brotherly affection! I don't, Olivia — because I *saw*!"

Swiftly she rose to her feet and came to face him.

"I never promised to give you my heart, Benedict. And I never pretended to love you — nor did you ask it of me. That was not part of the bargain. But I did promise to be faithful and dutiful, and that promise I shall keep as long as it is required of me. Luke is an old and dear friend, but you are my husband, and for that reason I owe you a loyalty I can give to no one else. If we have children, you can be sure that you alone could have fathered them. Is that not enough?''

His fine mouth hardened into a line of unyielding grimness; the blue eyes watching her were as cold as ice.

''It must be, I suppose,'' he conceded. He paused a moment, and then said: ''I am going to supper. You may join me if you wish.'' And he turned and left her.

She was not hungry, and she was tired and troubled and very miserable; but she did not want to give the servants cause for gossip. And above all she wanted somehow to repair the painful breach which had shattered all the carefully nourished warmth between them. After all, she had married him; there was no one else here at Spensley to whom she could turn.

So she splashed water on her face from the bowl in her dressing room, and tidied her hair, and went down to join him in the parlour. He greeted her with a cool 'good evening' as she took her seat, and then a long and uncomfortable silence enveloped them.

Olivia sat eating almost nothing, and now and then glancing nervously at the Earl. His face, with its perfect profile, its fine brows and brilliantly coloured eyes, the supple mouth which had kissed her so many times with a passion which set her body alight, was now a cold mask of severity, withdrawn, shutting her out. It was hard to believe he had ever smiled at her, or spoken to her softly or with tenderness. She was astonished to find how much she minded, how very close the pain was at his anger to what she had felt when she knew she had lost Luke. Yet that did not seem to make sense, for she had loved Luke all her life, as if he were truly a part of herself; and she neither loved nor respected the man she had married. Logically, she ought not to mind so much that he was angry with her. But she did mind, very much.

In the end she could bear it no longer. Somehow she must reach out to him, make him acknowledge her presence, touch him with some memory of the moments of happiness they had shared only a short time ago. She broke out: "I wish that this had not come between us. I meant no harm."

"You mean you wish I had not found out," he said nastily. "You did not expect me back so soon, did you?"

Olivia bent her head, biting her lip. So much for her attempt at peacemaking! She could not trust herself to say any more for fear of breaking down.

After a moment or two he went on in the same coldly distant tone:

"I found on reaching Oxford that I must go to London on business. I could have gone straight there. But I had a mind to spend a night with my wife on the way."

A night such as last night, she thought; or all the other nights of our marriage, filled with passion and delight. What would it be like now?

She discovered soon enough. After supper he shut himself in his little-used study, emerging very late after she herself had gone to bed. She had lain sleepless, very tired but staring unhappily into the shadowed folds of the bed canopy lit very dimly by the one candle left burning. Tonight the Earl brought his manservant with him, to help him undress and put his clothes away. On other nights she had undressed him as he her, making of it an extension of their lovemaking, an added delight. Now, once the man had gone, he came to bed without a word or a glance in her direction, extinguished the candle, and lay down a little apart from her with his back towards her. After a moment, she reached out a tentative hand to touch him, lightly caressing that unyielding back. He merely shrugged her off, and moved a little further away.

121

Olivia turned her face to the pillow and cried herself to sleep.

In the morning he was up and dressed before she woke, and had gone with a curt 'goodbye' before she was out of bed. She ran to the window and watched him ride away and prayed that he would come back soon and that somehow she would find a way to reconcile him to her.

The two weeks that followed were miserable ones. She thought she had known what it was to be lonely, but nothing she had ever felt before had been as bad as this. She tried to find ways to fill the long hours of his absence, but it seemed as if nothing could really occupy her full attention. Yet, once, she had thought that to be alone at Spensley would be the greatest happiness she could wish for. Even in visiting Tom's sick wife, and hearing their welcoming greetings, and their talk of old times, she could find no comfort. They seemed to talk as often of the young lord as of her father, and with an almost equal affection. That was another side of the man she had married to add to the puzzling whole: the kind and considerate master. They seemed to feel that her own influence as his wife was all that was needed to turn him into perfection itself. Olivia returned from her visits feeling more troubled and miserable than ever.

Once, she thought, she had rested on her memories of the past as a sure consolation in difficult times. Now there was, it seemed, no recollection that was safe from regret or pain. Even Luke, her friend — she dared not bring to mind any of that recent visit, for fear that she might have to face the implications of all he had said to her. Now the quarrel with her husband seemed more important and unbearable even than that.

Christmas Day came. In her father's house that day had never been marked out in any way; but Henry and Celia had always celebrated the twelve days of the festival with the most lavish festivities they could afford. Olivia had not found their idea of enjoyment – too much drink, ribald jokes and noisy parties – much to her taste, and had thought sometimes with longing of the country quiet of Spensley in winter time. Now, alone in that quietness, she wished for almost any distraction to make it bearable. The boughs with which the servants decked the rooms, the cheerfulness evident on their faces, the sense of excitement and anticipation, only made matters worse. She had no part in it, excluded as she was from any chance of happiness. After the disastrous end to that meeting with Luke she feared what might happen if he came again, and she did not want to deepen the rift between her husband and herself in any way. But she wished all the same that Luke would come and see her, so long as the meeting could be secret and unobserved. It would surely cheer her a little.

She was woken early on Christmas morning by the choir from the village church singing a carol beneath her window. She climbed out of bed and ran across the room to lean out and thank them, with tears in her eyes. She was deeply touched by the gesture, but it did not make her loneliness any easier to bear.

When they had gone, to be warmed on her instructions by some spiced ale in the kitchen, she dressed slowly and made her way through the adjoining rooms and onto the landing. At the head of the broad sweep of stairs she paused, trying to control her emotions before descending to face the servants, and the breakfast waiting for her.

'This is foolish,' she thought. 'Christmas meant nothing to me once. I should not mind being alone now. I should not feel it makes me more unhappy than ever.'

She heard someone come to the foot of the stairs, and hastily blew her nose and began calmly to descend; and then realised with a great lurching sensation which seemed to dislodge every organ in her body that the Earl was coming towards her. He was resplendent in the cinnamon satin he had worn on their wedding day; and he was smiling. She stood quite still.

A few steps below her he came to a halt, looking up at her. And then he said softly: "I misjudged you: I am sorry." And he held out his hand towards her.

Just for a moment she hesitated, and then she laid her hand in his, and he drew her down the last few steps into his arms.

He did not stay long at Spensley, even now. His presence was certainly required at court during the Christmas season, he told her; and as he felt that the King was beginning to soften towards their marriage it was all the more important that he should be there. This time though when he left her she no longer felt completely bereft — sad, yes, and she missed him, particularly during the long dark nights when her body ached for his touch and she wished she could reach out and feel him at her side. But there was a great deal to do, and now that she was happier she found real satisfaction in doing it. There was the house to oversee, of course; but he had entrusted her too in his absence with the day-to-day running of the estate, helped by his steward; and there were the plans for the gardens. Now at last she began to enjoy the feeling that Spensley was hers again, her home and her responsibility. She had made her choice, and though sometimes she would remember in a rush of unhappiness what might have been hers, and think of Luke and his distant farm, she schooled herself to accept what she had and make the best of it. She tried not to think at all of Luke's talk of plots. It seemed so unlikely, and now that the quarrel was over all seemed better than ever between the Earl and herself. He had, he said, found out a little about

Luke, and realised that what she had told him might very well be true. He had also learned of Luke's spell of imprisonment, and warned her against further contacts with him.

"Remember it's a very long time since you saw him last. People change. He keeps doubtful company — so take care."

'Luke warns me against Benedict, and Benedict against Luke,' she thought ruefully. 'Whose advice should I take?' But she did not argue with her husband. She was wary now of destroying his revived good humour. And she feared that after that last dreadful scene she was unlikely ever to see Luke again.

At the end of January the court returned to London, and the Earl spent two days at Spensley before joining them. They were happy days, happier, Olivia thought, than any in their marriage so far. Very slowly, the shyness between them was falling away, making more frequent the moments when she felt at ease in her husband's company. She wished very much that he was able to stay with her for a little longer. But she reminded herself that she had promised to be dutiful, and did not complain.

He left her, though, with one consolation of which he was quite unaware. Talking of the latest news of the progress of the war with the Dutch, he mentioned that the French had now allied themselves with England's enemy. It was a little while before the significance of the news reached Olivia; and when it did a great sense of relief swept her. Even if Luke had been right, and a faction at court plotted to use French help to force Catholicism on England, then that must surely now be at an end. If the French king had agreed to fight against his cousin King Charles there would be little point in trying to make some kind of secret treaty with him, for it would be doomed to failure. Watching her husband carefully,

125

Olivia was reassured by his calm cheerfulness. He did not look like a man who had just been thwarted in a plan dear to his heart. Luke must have been wrong.

The Earl did not return to Spensley until the end of March. But the weeks of his absence were not unhappy ones for Olivia. She had plenty to occupy her, especially as the days lengthened and spring came to the garden and the fields and woods; and there were two or three letters from her husband, full of lively news and tender messages. She need not fear yet, she thought, that he had tired of her. He told her often how much he longed to be with her, when once his court duties would allow.

But when he came home again it was once more for a brief two-day visit. And this time, though he seemed glad to see her, he was oddly preoccupied, silent and deep in thought for much of the time, or busy at some unknown work in his study. He had, he told her, seized the opportunity to be with her, but the King demanded his return to London as soon as possible. On the night before he left his lovemaking had a new urgency about it, almost as if he feared they might not be together again for a long time. But that, Olivia thought, was something she must not dwell upon. She parted from him tenderly next day, and tried to suppress the slight sense of unease she felt as the coach rolled away.

The very next day word was brought to her in the early evening that a man had come to Spensley seeking work, and insisted on speaking to her personally. He was a trained groom, he claimed, and he was waiting in the stable yard. Unconcerned, if a little puzzled, Olivia made her way to the yard, in darkness by now except where a lantern illuminated it, swinging and creaking in the chill wind. There was no one about, apart from the head groom standing beside a thin cloaked figure under the arch which led onto the road beyond. It was then that Olivia realised who it was.

She paused for a moment, gathering her thoughts against a fast beating heart. She felt a little tremor of anger that Luke should put her in this uncomfortable position. She loved him, and she would like above all to spend the rest of her life with him; but that was impossible, and for that reason it would be better if they did not meet.

However, he was here, so she drew a deep breath and went towards him.

"Ah, I know this man," she said to the head groom. "I'll attend to him. Go to your supper." She felt herself redden with shame at the deception, and as soon as he was out of earshot released her feelings on Luke. "Why did you come? We mustn't meet like this — it's all wrong!"

"How else can we meet? And I must see you. Surely you want that too?"

"Not if it forces me to deceive my husband."

"You don't love him."

"Luke, I *told* you —"

"I know, I know — you promised to be faithful and so on. I don't ask you to be anything else. After all, I saw clearly enough what kind of temper he has. But I must talk to you. It's urgent. Is there somewhere private?"

"Not where we might not be seen. It looks less deceitful if we talk here in the open, where we know if anyone's coming. No one will overhear us."

He seemed to be about to protest, but he thought better of it, and shrugged.

"As you wish. Only I want to hold you in my arms, and here I can't do that —" He caught sight of the distress on her face and said quickly: "I'm sorry. That's not what I came to say. I'll not waste time — you remember what I told you when I was here last — of a plot we suspected amongst the Catholic faction at court?"

"Yes," said Olivia, "but the French are openly our enemies now. You need not fear that any more."

"Did I not tell you it was a secret plan? All the better for them if openly we are at war. And it's quite clear that the French are offering little material help to the Dutch. I do not believe their hearts are in it. No, we have all the more reason to fear — for we know now that what we suspected was true. There *is* a plot — and we are almost certain that your husband is in the very thick of it, perhaps its instigator."

Olivia found herself shivering.

"That's nonsense, Luke — it must be. He's not like that. He's not a serious man, not even about religion. It's fashionable to be a Catholic at court, that's all. And he cares too much for his own skin to risk anything so dangerous. Think of the disgrace — or worse — if he should be found out!"

"That's just what we have thought of. And when we have the proof we need we shall expose all those who have a hand in it for the traitors they are. But we must have firm proofs — no one will believe us without them, for all those involved are powerful men in favour at court. Will you help us, Olivia?"

"Help you!" Astonishment gave force to her voice, and Luke reached out in alarm to silence her. He waited a moment or two to be sure no one came to investigate the sudden noise before he went on: "Yes. For you are in an ideal position to search the Earl's belongings here for any signs of his treachery."

"*His* treachery! — What of mine, if I were to do that to my husband? How can you even suggest such a thing?"

"I thought there were some principles you held more highly than loyalty to such a man. You are your father's daughter, are you not? What would he have done, do you think?"

"Not this, I'm quite sure," she replied with emphasis. "He was honourable too."

128

"Olivia, the nation is in deadly danger — you *must* put that first, above every other loyalty."

"You only tell me it's in deadly danger. I have no reason to think so otherwise. There is nothing in my husband's behaviour or his actions to lead me to think there is anything in what you say."

"He does not spend very much time here with you, does he?"

"How do you know that?" she asked sharply.

"We have him watched." At her little indignant cry he said calmly, "How else can we hope to find proof? We must leave no avenue unexplored. You can be sure we have a much better idea of his movements than you have. As to where he is now, for example —"

Olivia shuddered, suddenly afraid.

"I don't want to know."

Luke held her arm. "Where did he tell you he was going? To London, to the court, I suppose? Come now, admit it."

"He would not lie to me."

"How do you know? You don't really know him as well as that, do you? Shall I tell you where he is? I know, for a friend of mine is following him. I hope the sea's not too rough, for he's not a good sailor — my friend, I mean. Your husband seems to be able to face a voyage at any time of year without trouble."

Olivia knew that the colour had drained from her face. It was no use now to pretend that he had not surprised her.

"You'd better tell me exactly what you mean," she said.

"He *is* going to court, Olivia — but to the French court, for secret talks with King Louis — or so our information leads us to believe. Our informant is very reliable. It is not his first visit, by the way. We hope this time that in following him we will be able to lay our hands on some documentary proof of his activities — or some sworn witness who will be

129

believed. If we fail there will, I think, be other oppor-
tunities. I hope so, for we must succeed in the end
— for the sake of us all. Do you see that now?"

Olivia half-turned from him, averting her eyes.

"I . . . I don't know," she faltered. "I don't know
what to think."

"If you find proof amongst his papers you will
know. And if you find nothing you can do no harm.
Will you do that for us?"

"No!" she burst out. "No, that I can't do! I promised — Luke, please understand!"

In the end she convinced him, though it was hard,
and the effort left her exhausted and close to tears.
She was relieved at least that he did seem to understand finally that whatever her husband had done —
even if what Luke said were true — she could not set
herself to spy on him.

She knew, though, that in another sense Luke had
won, for his very urgency convinced her that there
must be something in what he said. Either that, or
her friend was out of his mind, turned by suffering to
believe that an enemy lurked in every corner. She did
not want to believe that, any more than that her husband was a fanatical traitor. It seemed that whichever
way she turned there was no comfort to be found.

Before he left Luke put her on her guard.

"Olivia, I am afraid for you. Once he has what he
wants he'll have no more need of a Puritan wife to
give him respectability. Your usefulness will be over.
Perhaps he will be able to claim that your marriage
was invalid, as a Papist priest conducted it. That
would be the best, for you would be free — and I
shall be here still. But it may be he will find simpler
means of freeing himself —" His eyes looked very
black in his grave face, black and full of fear for her.
"He is a ruthless man at heart, whatever he may seem.
He will stop at nothing. Have a care — and come to
me at once if you fear for your safety. Promise me

130

that?"

She promised, scarcely understanding him but chilled by the conviction in his voice.

When he had gone, kissing her once, lightly and swiftly, and promising, though she protested, to come again, she did not immediately go back into the house. Instead she wandered into the garden and sat on a seat close to where, in daylight, the grass was golden with daffodils; and tried to make some sense of all Luke had said.

He had sounded so sure. Hearing him, she had found herself believing what he said. But now he had gone she did not know what to think. She had only his word, set against her growing knowledge of her husband. And that knowledge was, as yet, slight and contradictory. He did not behave towards her like a man who saw her only as a convenient cover for his secret activities. Much more was he like the man she imagined him to be, infatuated by her body, deeply attracted to her, as he would be to a mistress, his passion for her still alive and real. If he was a little stiff with her in the daytime, that was only to be expected, for he was, she guessed, not very interested in her as a person, but only as a bedfellow.

What else was there, she wondered, which might give her a clue to the truth? He was jealous, knowing she had never pretended to love him and fearing perhaps that he might lose her before he had tired of her. Yet he was kindly and attentive, when he was at Spensley. And he had never promised to spend more time with her than at court. His duty lay at court — and his pleasures, apart from her.

Only one small thing seemed to bear out what Luke had told her: his mood at their parting yesterday. But that was nothing, so slight that she might have imagined it. He had not taken much luggage with him when he left, and he had been dressed as if for court. It was Luke's word against his.

But she knew Luke well, and he her, and he had never been less than completely honest with her. Could she say the same of the Earl?

On impulse she went then, quickly, to Benedict's study, that small orderly room where once her father too had worked. She shut the door firmly behind her and stood looking round, with a sense of shame mingled with fear. What if she were to find something that told her that everything Luke had said was true? She knew that whatever else she found, she did not want that.

But she searched all the same, as if she could not help herself, as if she had to know. With swift careful fingers she opened boxes and drawers and glanced swiftly through the papers stored there: bills and receipts, letters on estate matters — he had told her they were kept here — legal documents. Folded carefully inside a book she found a letter in French — and knew enough to realise very soon that it had been written, long ago, by Queen Henrietta Maria, the King's mother, to Benedict's mother, wishing her a speedy recovery, and promising to care for her infant son. Lady Alston must, Olivia supposed, have died soon afterwards; and the Queen had, in her fashion, kept her promise. But the letter held no clue to that son's present actions.

There was no other clue either. She searched with a thoroughness Luke would have commended, and found nothing at all to bear out his accusations. With a great feeling of relief she went at last to supper.

It was not so easy though to set her mind completely at rest. Time and again through the weeks that followed she found herself wondering what she ought to believe. She longed for one of her husband's light-hearted, loving letters, full of court gossip, but none came. Did that mean he was too busy to write? Or that he had found more agreeable female company at court? Or that he was too far away on too secret a mission to be able to write? 'Please let it not be that!' she prayed.

A warm dry spring led almost imperceptibly into a hot dry summer, and still there was no news of the Earl, nor did he return. It was June now, and the hay was ready for cutting. Long ago, when affairs of state permitted, Olivia's father had loved to help with harvest and haymaking, working alongside his men; and she too had joined him, enjoying the sun and fresh air, the steady, tiring, satisfying work, the songs of the men and women as they worked, the pauses for rest and refreshment and laughter in the shade of the great trees fringing the fields, the joyous celebration afterwards.

Now, as mistress of Spensley, she dressed herself in a worn blue holland gown, tied her hair back with a ribbon and set off at dawn with her labourers to work with them until darkness brought the toil to an end. The long days were full of activity, leaving no time to think, the nights short and lost in exhausted sleep. And she enjoyed the companionship of her fellow workers, whole families together, eager as she was to see the hay safely dried and carted and stored before the weather broke.

There had been three days of work and the sun was hotter than ever. At Olivia's orders barrels of ale were brought out to the fields at noon and rolled under the trees where the workers sank down to rest. There was beef, too, and bread, which she found as welcome as they did. She sat down on the grass beside the miller's wife and her three children, and ate hungrily, and then lay back with closed eyes, hearing the slow talk about her, the quiet laughter, the gentle rustle of the wind in the trees.

She must have fallen asleep after a time, for she woke with a start when the miller's wife nudged her sharply.

"My lady — look!" She sat up quickly. Coming

across the field in the full hot sunlight, his hair gleaming silver fair, his skin bronzed, his shoulders broad in his silk shirt — he wore no doublet — was the Earl himself, come home at last.

Olivia scrambled to her feet and ran swiftly over the stubble towards him. And there in full view of the smiling haymakers she fell into his arms, and his mouth came down on hers as if there at last he found all the refreshment he needed.

She had forgotten completely where they were, and that they were not alone. She felt his hands run over her body, firm and urgent through the thin fabric. She felt desire sweep her with a depth and a power that took from her any thought but of his nearness. She heard him whisper "Come home — now!" and went with him without a second thought. It was almost more than she could bear to wait so long before they reached their room, and the bed, and could fall together into its softness to find each other again.

Afterwards, as she lay sleepily against him, she felt him give a deep sigh which echoed her own sense of utter contentment.

"It's good to be home," he said softly. "This time I shall stay longer, God willing." She felt his hand run over her hair. "There's hay in your hair."

She laughed, and hugged him. All the fears and uncertainties of the past months seemed very far away, banished and out of reach. She was only glad that he was home. But even so, probing a little perhaps, she could not resist saying: "The King's had more than his share of your company this year. You must be back in his favour."

"Very soon you'll be welcome at court too," he agreed. "You will put all the other ladies to shame." And he turned to kiss her again.

Much later they went together to see how the haymaking was progressing, and she showed him the

new plants in the garden, and they had supper together there as the sun sank low in the sky. The night
that followed was as sweet as Olivia could have
desired.

Next morning he left her sleeping while he took a
turn in the fields. She rose late, and dressed slowly,
lazy with happiness and physical contentment.

The Earl had left his doublet of yesterday flung
over a chair, and she smoothed the heavy creased
silk; and then noticed on the floor beneath the chair
a crumpled piece of paper. It must, she supposed,
have fallen from a pocket. She bent to pick it up,
idly glancing at it as she did so.

It was a bill of recent date for a night's stay at an
inn, with supper and breakfast and stabling for a
horse. And it was written in French.

NINE

Olivia stood for what seemed a very long time staring at the paper and feeling a deadly chill steal through her limbs, turning her happiness to ice, destroying hope and trust in one horrible step. Then, as if she had come suddenly awake, she crushed it fiercely and flung it into the empty hearth and grasped the tinder box and struck a flame; and watched until the paper was nothing but a tiny scattering of ash.

She did not know why she had done it. She had destroyed the one piece of firm and irrefutable evidence that Luke had been right, that her husband had indeed been in France. And in so doing she had not — and could not — destroy her knowledge of that fact. But it was as if she wanted at once to remove any possibility that she might one day pass the paper to Luke to supply the evidence he sought.

She had just risen to her feet again and was standing gazing down at the black remnants when the door opened and the Earl came in. She turned sharply, guiltily aware of the faint and lingering smell of burning.

He was smiling, at ease; but one look at her face brought him in concern to her side.

"What's wrong, Olivia? You look very pale. Are you ill?"

Dumbly, unable to think of any reply, she shook her head. Surely she ought to say now: "Luke was here. He said you were in France. And I know he was right. Please tell me that the rest of what he said was untrue, that he's wrong about the kind of man you are."

136

But she could not say it. She knew already how angry he would be if she told him Luke had been to Spensley again. She could only guess at how he would react if he knew what else she thought of him. If only she could have been sure — or almost sure — that he would deny the charges, and reassure her with some simple and reasonable explanation of his actions, and of the tell-tale bill. But she was instead very nearly certain that he would not be able to do so. Even more, she was all at once deeply afraid of his reaction if indeed he were guilty as Luke said. Luke believed she was in danger. If the Earl knew she had seen evidence of his guilt, and was in a position to send word of it to Luke, might he not take some terrible, unimaginable step to see that she could not do so? Or might he not at least guess at Luke's part in the affair, and act against him before he could find out any more?

Olivia felt sick, cold with fear and uncertainty. When the Earl laid a gentle hand on her shoulder she almost recoiled, so afraid of him was she all at once. Yet she must not let him guess what she thought. She held her head high and forced a smile and said in what was meant to be a light tone but sounded hard and frightened: "I am tired, I think — I shall walk in the garden. The air will do me good."

He drew her to his side, and she let him do so, though she did not lean against him as once she would have done.

"You must rest today then. No work in the fields. I shall take care of you."

She was tempted to say: "Leave me alone — go away and leave me in peace!" But that would only require more explanation.

The following weeks, which should have been so happy, were a time of torment to Olivia. This time her husband kept his word and stayed for a long while at Spensley, devoting his attention to her as often as he could. It did not take him long to realise that something more than simple fatigue was troubling his wife. Though she tried desperately to act as normally as possible towards him, Olivia found she could not put from her mind her fears and suspicions. She knew her coldness hurt him. More than once he begged her to tell him what was wrong. And more than once she was sorely tempted to tell him. But fear of his reaction always kept her silent. And in time he grew irritated by what he saw as her sulkiness, and turned cold in his turn. Illogically, that hurt her, though it made it easier for her to live with what she knew. She longed for someone to talk to — even Luke, though unfairly perhaps she blamed him in some obscure way for this new rift in her marriage.

The hay was safely in, and then the corn. The Earl and Countess concealed their differences to appear at the festivities and rejoice at the good harvest. Olivia forced herself also to play the part of the smiling hostess on the two occasions when they had guests at Spensley. But each occasion only served in the end to deepen her suspicions.

The first time the guest was James Fontwell, with another man she did not know. They came for dinner and for supper, and the meals passed in light talk, as if they none of them had a care in the world. But throughout the afternoon and much of the night the men were shut in the Earl's study, deep in conversation, and Olivia observed that her husband's mood that day, and for some time afterwards, was thoughtful and withdrawn.

James Fontwell was also among the second group of visitors, as was the other man. But this time there were two others and the wife of one of them, tall and fair and beautiful, but cool in her manner towards Olivia. She, like the men, was admitted to the long discussions in the study. When, once, Olivia plucked up courage to knock on the door and ask if perhaps they required refreshment, she could see that her husband was angry at the interruption. He told her curtly that they had all they needed and must not be disturbed, and she hurried away, trembling at the coldness she had seen in his eyes.

The next day, he informed her, without warmth or concern, that he must go to court again, and his kiss at parting was cool and light and meaningless. It was a long time, she realised, since he had come to her with anything approaching passion. Yet she could not complain, for it was her doing as much as his. She found herself wishing, miserably, that Luke had never come back, and then scolded herself for her unfairness. After all, if her husband was a dangerous traitor it was better that she should know.

It chilled her to find how soon after her husband's departure Luke came to see her. They must still be watching his every movement. Luke must have been keeping an eye on her, too, for he came to her as she set out on horseback to ride to the house of a tenant with some problem which required attention. She had ridden only a few yards from the house when Luke called out from a spinney near the road.

She reined in the horse but did not dismount, waiting until he came up to her.

"I wish you would not come," she said, aware even as she spoke that she was being churlish. For had he not been right in the end?

"I had to," he replied, his voice low and urgent. "You must come away with me at once."

"Why?" she asked sharply.

"Their plan is almost complete. When it is then you will be in the greatest possible danger. You will be safe with me."

"I thought you meant to expose them so they couldn't carry out their plan?"

"So we do. But not until they have embroiled themselves up to the hilt. There must be no room for doubt in any minds —"

"I thought you were sure!"

"*We* are sure. But we must be able to convince others. Did I not tell you that? — Can you come at once, Olivia?"

She did not know why she shook her head with such vehemence.

"No, I cannot."

"Why ever not? — Olivia, the plan is likely to reach fruition in the next week or two, even before. We're waiting for word of the final rendezvous. I must have you safe before then."

She shook her head more firmly than ever.

"No, Luke, no! I shall know when there's danger — I'll come then. But not now." He reached up and grasped the horse's bridle, and she cried out in anger. "Leave me, Luke! I make my own decisions. I know what I'm doing. If you like, tell me where to find you if I should need you. And then go. Someone might see us, and then there'll be trouble for both of us."

In the end he had to accept that he could not move her. He gave her the address of the wealthy London Puritan in whose house he was staying — ostensibly working as a clerk — and then stood back to let her go. She rode away, and realised as she did so that she was weeping. She could never marry Luke now; but he had made it impossible for her to find happiness with anyone else. Just at this moment, with complete unreasonableness, she thought she was close to hating him.

Benedict came back the following evening. He looked tired and anxious, and his careworn appearance almost moved her to pity. She had to restrain a longing to hold him in her arms and comfort him. But he found some comfort that night, turning to her in the dark as if his hunger for her could no longer go unsatisfied. And she found herself responding to him in forgetfulness of everything but her need for him.

Just for that little time they were together again.

But it was not as it had been, for afterwards he fell instantly asleep, and the next morning he was as cool towards her as ever. He was busy with some business of his own during the morning, and she did not see him again until he came to her room just before dinner. She turned her head as he closed the door, and recognised with a sense of dread that a cold fury had him in its grasp.

"So! Now I know why you've turned so cold, wife. That old friend enjoys you now, does he? So much for your fidelity!"

She rose to her feet and faced him.

"No, that's quite untrue. There's never been anyone but you."

"You as good as told me once that you loved him. Do you deny he's been here several times since then, in secret, in my absence?"

How did he know? She opened her mouth to reply, but no words came. After a moment he answered her unspoken question.

"You thought you would not be found out, didn't you? But some of my household are loyal, if you are not. You were seen yesterday — and the man who saw you remembered another occasion when you'd been together a long time in the stable yard. Dear God!" he broke out, "almost under my own roof! How could you? Did you use our bed as well? Have you no shame?"

"Why do you have to believe the worst of me? He came without my knowledge or approval — we talked, and I told him to go, and not to come again — that's all."

"What did he want then? Is he some kind of spy?"

He took a step nearer and grasped her arm, and she felt herself go white.

"I don't know what you mean — Let me go, you're hurting!"

141

He did so, but thrust her from him so roughly that she almost fell.

"God, what did I do when I married you? I was a fool, a blind besotted fool — I should have known no good would come of it. You're a Puritan to the soul and always will be — your father's daughter, every inch of you —"

"And proud of it!" she shot back at him.

"Don't I know it! Only you married me, God help us both, and that your father's daughter should never have done. Your heart was never in it, was it? And you knew your mistake after the first days. You gave up then. There was never any hope for us."

"Hope? What hope did you have? That I'd be a quiet uncomplaining little wife keeping your bed warm while you danced the time away at court? A mistress in all but name — that's what you wanted, wasn't it? A kept woman!"

"You were glad enough to be kept, if it looked legal. Yes, you're right, that's what you are, isn't it — a whore in all but name? Only now it seems you want the name too. Is he good in bed this Luke? As good as I was once, before you turned cold on me? And of course he's a Puritan too, like you. Do you talk sedition in bed, afterwards? That must add a little spice to —"

"Don't!" she cried suddenly, pressing her hands to her ears. "Don't talk like that! You're wrong — wrong! Oh, he came here, that's true, and I did not tell you — I was afraid —"

"You had cause to be! Deceitful, lying woman!"

"I did not lie to you! Not like you did to me. You did not tell me you went to France, did you? All that time when I thought you were at court —"

There was a complete silence. He stood very still, staring at her, his face pale, for what seemed a very long time. She watched him, and thought: 'I should not have said that — I did not mean to.'

Then he came and grasped both her arms.

"What do you mean?" he hissed. "What are you saying?"

She dared not meet his eyes.

"You . . . when you came back . . . I found a bill, in French, in our room, fallen on the floor — you said you had been in London . . ."

After a moment she felt his grasp slacken. He drew a deep breath and then said unsteadily. "Why did you say nothing?"

She was afraid to tell him the extent of her suspicions. She faltered, "I . . . I don't know —"

"You had no reason to suppose it was my bill, had you? Might not someone have given it to me? And if I was in France, so what? Do I have to account for all my actions to you? I lived there for years — I have friends there still. May a man not visit his friends?" His grip tightened again momentarily. "Did you talk of this to anyone?" There was a dangerous edge to his voice. She raised her eyes to his face so that he could read there the truthfulness of her reply.

"No. I told no one." Thank goodness she had said nothing to Luke about the note!

He gazed at her intently for a moment or two longer, and then his hands fell and he said abruptly: "Come to dinner. We'll talk afterwards."

She knew he meant her to come with him at once, but she hesitated.

"Let me tidy myself first. I'll join you soon."

She thought he would insist she came immediately, but he did not. When he had gone she went to the window and sank down on the window seat and was astonished to find how much she was trembling.

'We'll talk afterwards,' he had said, and she did not like the gravity of his tone, as if there was to be something momentous in the talk. Perhaps it was not a talk he planned at all, but something else. He knew now that she had found out some of what he had kept hidden from her. Would he guess that Luke was working against him, and suppose that she was in league with her old friend? After all, he knew Luke had doubtful associates; he had warned her against them.

She wished suddenly that she had gone with Luke the other day. She would be safe in London now, away from this horrible uncertainty, the sense that nothing was sure, that nothing was as it seemed; that she might indeed be in deadly danger.

And she would be far away too from this marriage for which once she had held some faint hope. and which now in all but name was over, finished. It had been founded on passion, and passion was at an end. There was nothing left. Better far that she admitted that, and turned her back on it before any more pain was wasted on it.

For beneath all her fear and her suspicion lay a deep and horrible pain. It was a pain of loss: loss of happiness, loss of love. She had hoped that these two things might grow from the passion of those early days of marriage. Perhaps the Earl's secret plans had always made that impossible; but once it had not seemed so. Once indeed it had seemed as if she could learn not to regret that Luke had come back too late, and not to feel that what she had was second best. But that hope had gone now, long since. In going with Luke she might have been able to salvage something from the confusion and muddle of her life, and the man she left behind might also have been able to begin again, with someone else.

She came then to a decision, and once it was made she acted quickly. She packed a few essentials in a bag, dressed in her riding clothes and moved towards the door. Then, on impulse, she went to her writing desk, pulled paper and pen towards her and wrote:

Don't come after me. When I want you to contact

me, I will let you know. Try and find a way to end
our marriage. You will be happier without me.

And then she made her way down the back stair
to the stables.

TEN

It was almost exactly a year since Olivia had left London, and it was a very different city to which she returned. Gone was the dreadful eerie emptiness, and in its place now was the city she knew of old: vulgar, raucous, colourful, the narrow crowded streets close and stinking in the mid-August heat.

She reached London in the morning two days after her flight from Spensley. Fearful of being followed, she had avoided the highways, and more than once lost her way. At night she slept under hedges, cramped and stiff from her ride, always hungry because she dared not go openly to an inn to eat. She had been too miserable to care greatly about the discomfort of it all.

Tired as she was, it took her some time to find Luke's lodgings in a large and prosperous house not far from the Strand. When she learned on reaching it that Luke was not at home she sank against the doorpost and gave way to helpless tears.

Abel Whiting, the merchant whose house it was, was a kindly man and wasted no time in wondering who this strange woman might be. Olivia found herself helped indoors, comforted and fed and conducted very soon to a soft and comfortable bed. She slept deeply for a long time.

When she woke a girl seated at the bedside helped her to dress and led her downstairs to a small booklined study; and there, working at a table by the window, was Luke.

He looked up as she came in, and then with an exclamation sprang to his feet and took her in his arms. And the next moment he had pressed his mouth to hers and was kissing her with a sudden feverish passion.

Olivia, in the first instant thankful only to be safe, all at once found herself struggling to be free. There was no answering flame in her, no passion or excitement. She was glad enough to be held with brotherly tenderness — but she did not want this, the self-same demanding fire which in her husband had so often and so surely set her alight.

Aware of her unresponsiveness, Luke drew away at last. "What's wrong? May I not kiss you?"

"I . . . I'm tired," she said weakly, troubled at her own coldness, almost ashamed. After all, had the choice been offered to her freely, she would have married Luke. "Besides, I am still another man's wife."

"Then we must do all we can to have your marriage set aside as soon as possible. It's a good thing you were married by a Popish priest — that must make it easier. It will be invalid I think — or if not, then a Papist with influence can get an annulment without difficulty, I believe."

Gently she pushed him from her and turned away.

"It doesn't seem right," she murmured. "I promised, after all — and I meant it then —"

"Of course you did. But if you have made a grave mistake, then you must try and put it right. You remember that pamphlet Mr John Milton wrote on the subject of divorce? He held that it was a desirable alternative to living in misery. I'm sure he was right."

"My father didn't —"

"Your father was happy in his marriage. Think, Olivia, you can be free again!"

'Free,' she thought dully. 'Free for what?' Free to live a quiet orderly respectable life; free to turn her back on confusion, danger, uncertainty. Free of those nights of wild passion, of the touch that set her body

147

on fire, the grief of parting, the joy of reunion —

Free to marry again, to marry Luke, the love of her life.

She turned to look at him, studying the dark features, the lean awkward frame, the small mouth which just now had failed to bring an answering kiss from her; and she felt nothing. She might have been looking at a stranger.

But that was ridiculous. 'I must be tired,' she thought. 'Tomorrow, when I'm rested, I shall feel differently.' She smiled wanly. "We'll talk about it later," she said. And then she tried, with unexpected difficulty, to tell him why she had come. She could not understand why she felt so reluctant, disloyal almost, when she explained the paper she had found, the secretive visits, the long weeks of fear and uncertainty and that final dreadful quarrel. She was glad at least that Luke readily accepted the story, as simply confirming what he knew already.

"I'm sure you left only just in time," he said at last. "Things must be coming to a head — he's in London again, you know."

She felt her heart give a great leap.

"In London! Now? When did he come? Where is he?"

'Perhaps he's come for me,' she thought. 'Perhaps he wants to make up our differences, as he did after that first quarrel.'

"He's at Alston House at present — you know, his London house. He arrived last night. The other conspirators have been calling there. We are watching him, of course. And waiting for word from a close contact of them all, who will let us know what moves they will make, and when. There is a messenger expected soon from France."

So very likely he was not even thinking of her. Olivia bent her head and wished the reflection could have given her some comfort. After all, she had fled from him in fear for her life, had she not?

She wandered to a chair at the far side of the room, and sat down, heavily. Misunderstanding her dejected mood, Luke came and took her hand.

"It will all be over very soon, Olivia," he comforted her. "Then you can put the past behind you and start again. We can both start again."

She could not hurt him by telling him that his words gave her no comfort at all.

Next day she saw little of Luke. They ate breakfast together with the merchant and his family for company, and soon afterwards he went out. She did not ask, but she knew his absence had something to do with her husband.

Once he had gone, Olivia went in search of Mr Whiting.

"I borrowed a horse from Spensley to bring me here," she told him. "I'd like to return it somehow to Alston House. It does after all belong to my husband. But I don't want him to know where it comes from."

Mr Whiting smiled faintly.

"Do you not think he can afford to let you keep one horse for yourself? You'll hardly be robbing him of anything he values very much. From the look of the beast it can't exactly have been the pride of his stable."

Olivia coloured and bent her head.

"I want to owe him nothing — nothing at all," she said with vehemence. The merchant did not argue the point any further; and duly made arrangements for the horse to be left, as discreetly as possible, in the stable yard of Alston House. For a moment Olivia found herself imagining that her husband, seeing the horse, would somehow trace her whereabouts and come to beg her to return. But she suppressed the vision: after all, it was not something she could possibly want to happen.

It was a restless and uncomfortable day. She had nothing with which to occupy herself, and the merchant's wife declined all offers of help, urging her to rest. She tried to read, taking first one book and then another from the study shelves and turning the pages without enthusiasm. It seemed as if nothing today could distract her from wondering what Luke was doing, and where her husband was, and what would come of it all.

When Luke came home after supper she went to him at once, eager for news. But one glance at his face made her catch her breath in fear. She had never seen quite that look in his eyes before: dismay, apprehension, horror almost.

"What's wrong?" she asked sharply, oblivious of the presence in the room of their host and his wife.

"I must talk to you alone," Luke said abruptly, and drew her with him into the study, closing the door firmly behind him. Then he told her: "There's been a change of plan."

She looked at him questioningly, waiting for him to go on, but he said nothing more, simply gazing gloomily into the empty hearth.

"Aren't you going to tell me?" she prompted at last, and he looked up as if he was surprised to hear her speaking.

"Of course — Olivia, we found we could not lay our hands on the evidence we needed —"

So *that* was why he looked so gloomy! She felt her heart give a great leap with relief, and tried to prevent a smile of foolish delight from spreading across her face.

"Then he is not implicated in anything."

"I didn't say that. We have no doubt of that, Olivia." His tone was severe, reproving almost. "Unfortunately, they've covered their tracks well. They leave no traces. What a pity you burnt that bill! — Though perhaps by itself it would not have been

150

enough." He came to face her. "You see, Olivia, we cannot rely on sworn witnesses alone. However honest they are they will not be believed against men so powerful. We need concrete evidence if we are to bring the conspiracy to light. That is what is so frustrating – we know of the plot, we know every detail, or all that matters. We know there have been talks in France about using French help to turn England Catholic, in return for English support for French ambitions in Europe. We know, moreover, that Lord Alston is without doubt the main instigator of the plot, and the chief contact with France. We know that without him the whole scheme would fall apart, so central is he to its success. And we know that the final contacts are to be made tomorrow night, when he goes to meet an agent near Dover in a ruined farmhouse they have used before. After that, it will be too late to put a stop to it all, without the firm evidence we have not been able to find." He paused again. Olivia studied his face, grim and frowning. He looked like a man who saw the end of all his hopes, and gazed into a future where the evil he was powerless to destroy would take shape unhindered by anything he could do. Yet some instinct told Olivia that this alone did not explain the lurking horror in his eyes, that there was something more, something worse, which he could not bring himself to tell her. When he spoke again, it seemed to be in such a different tone that she was startled.

"Come with me, Olivia. We'll go tonight, to Holland first, and then to America."

"Then you're giving up?" she asked. "You don't even want to stay and fight, if it comes to that?"

"Not when the weapons are –" he broke off abruptly. "Pack your things. We should go at once, as soon as we can."

"I don't understand," she said slowly.

"Why not? It's clear enough. I told you about the

farm. We shall go there — you will be happy there, I know —"

"But I am married still."

"You won't . . . that doesn't matter. America's a long way off. No one will know — and if they did —" He stopped again, and then said: "It will be all right, Olivia. Believe me, it will."

An inexplicable chill crept along her spine. There was that look in his eyes again, which hinted at something he dared not say aloud. It seemed to belie all the reassurance in his words.

"What's happened, Luke? Why must we go so suddenly? Have you been found out?" She remembered with a tremor that Lord Alston knew of her links with Luke. Had he realised how Luke was working against him, and taken steps to put an end to that threat? In running to Luke, had she put her old friend in grave danger?

"Not that I know of," he said. "But after tomorrow night —" A pleading note came into his voice. "Just take my word for it that we must go. Come with me."

"Will your friends come too?" She saw at once that she had touched on the heart of the trouble, for his eyes seemed to darken, bleaker than ever.

"They — no — we have parted company."

She could stand it no longer.

"Luke, tell me what's wrong! I know you're keeping something from me. Have you quarrelled with the others?"

"No, it's not that. But I find I cannot work with them any more. I cannot work with them, yet I cannot work against them. So I must go, at once." As if he hoped for some reassurance that he was right, he said earnestly, "You believe, don't you, that you cannot put right a wrong by doing something evil? That if you do you only bring yourself down to their level — to the level of those who are doing wrong?"

152

"Of course." She spoke calmly, but a new and horrible fear was taking shape within her. "Luke, what are they planning?"

He hesitated, then answered her in a whisper. "Murder."

Somewhere, following some instinct deeper than conscious thought, a little voice cried 'Oh, my dear!' and she knew it was not Luke for whom she feared. She stood very still, waiting.

"They say that to expose him, even if it were possible, would only thwart him for the moment. That even if he fails this time he might yet plot again, one day, with more success. They say — and I know they are right — that without him the whole thing will come to nothing, even at this late stage. If he does not live to bring word to the King the day after tomorrow, and see the plan brought to fruition, then the danger will be past."

Olivia did not need to ask who 'he' was. White to the lips she heard every whispered word as if Luke had shouted it from the rooftops, and each one struck through her as if it were a blow to the heart.

"They are right, Olivia. They have reason on their side. But I cannot have a part in it."

In sudden fierce anguish, no longer remotely concerned with Luke's troubled feelings, she cried out: "Then don't let them do it — warn him — put him on his guard! You can do that, can't you?"

"And betray my friends?"

"You don't have to do that — just tell him enough to protect him."

"It would come to the same thing. Use your head, Olivia! If he's forewarned he'll have armed men waiting for them, you know that. I can't let that happen."

"So you'd allow the innocent to suffer!"

"Innocent!" Luke exploded. "He's not innocent! He's up to his neck in conspiracy. He'd have us plunged into bloodshed and civil war again if he had

153

his way. He'd have no mercy on any who stood in his way — even you, his own wife. I cannot care what becomes of him — he deserves the very worst. But for all that I cannot have a hand in his murder, for in doing that I should stoop to his level. You cannot build a new and better world on conspiracy and murder."

"So you'll run away and let him die, to keep your hands clean?"

"What else can I do, tell me that? These men are my friends — I owe them my silence at least, not to make things worse. Come with me — I know you hate the thought of it as much as I do, but we can do nothing — and once it's over we'll be free to be together."

"Luke!" The name was wrung from her like a cry of pain. "How can you! He is my husband — I don't care what he's done —" She reached out and grasped his arms, shaking him. "Tell me what they plan — tell me so I can warn him — they are not *my* friends."

He pulled himself free.

"Olivia, he would think nothing of killing you!"

She knew then with sudden complete certainty that Luke was wrong. He might be right in everything else he told her, but in that he had misjudged the Earl completely: he would never do her any harm. But if she did not move quickly he himself would be in deadly danger.

"You are wrong, Luke, I know you are wrong. Go if you must — but I shall not come with you. I am going to warn him before it's too late —" As she ran from the room she heard Luke's protesting cry following her, but she took no notice at all. Just as she was, she rushed into the streets, already shadowed with evening. She had no thought for her own safety, no fear of what might happen to her, alone, in these lawless streets. Her one goal was to reach Alston House and warn her husband of his danger. There was so little time.

It was not far to the fine riverside mansions of the nobility. Alston House stood behind high walls in the Strand, just as she had imagined it when Benedict had described it to her. Only in her mind she had seen it bright with candles, full of music and light female laughter. Now it was dark and shuttered and firmly barred against intruders, like a house empty and deserted. In a sudden panic she grasped the high wrought-iron gates and rattled them fiercely, calling for help.

After what seemed an age a burly man came, cudgel in hand, to the gate, a barking dog at his heels.

"What's going on there?"

Would he believe her if she drew herself to her full height and said: "Let me in. I am Lady Alston"? She could almost imagine the disbelieving and scornful laughter that would bring. Instead she said quickly: "I must see Lord Alston. Now, at once — it is a matter of the greatest urgency."

"It'll have to wait then," said the man. "My lord's out of town. Won't be back until the day after tomorrow. Good night, wench."

She did not even try to convince him that she was the Countess of Alston; but something in her tone must have persuaded him that she was in deadly earnest, for in the end he told her all he knew. It was little enough: that my lord had gone south — into Kent the man thought — and had left on horseback attended by a single manservant. Perhaps, the man suggested, he had gone hunting.

"My lord doesn't talk about his plans, wench. He'll not have let anyone know — always supposing he knew himself. You'll just have to wait until the day after tomorrow."

And by then he would be dead, murdered by Luke's friends. Unless she could reach him first.

Olivia stood staring blankly at the mansion long after the man had gone, asking herself what on earth

155

she could do now. She had been sure she would find him here. And now she had no idea where he was, or where to begin looking for him. She did not even know any details of the planned murder. She guessed that they meant to surprise him at the rendezvous near Dover — in a ruined farmhouse, Luke had said — and she supposed that it would be tomorrow night. But that was all. Was she to search the whole Dover area single-handed for a likely ruin, and hope it would be the right one?

'I would even do that, if there were no other way,' she thought. But it would take so long — too long. It was already dark, and close on midnight. That left at most twelve hours, twelve short hours in which to save a man from certain death. In that time she could barely hope to reach Dover, even riding without a break; and there would be no time for a search.

Her only hope — a slender, fragile one — was to go back to Luke and make him, somehow, tell her all he knew of the planned murder — where, and when, and how. But in telling her he would be betraying his friends. He would not willingly do that to save a man who had taken from him the woman he loved. Only, there was nothing else she could do.

She set out at a run back to the merchant's house, to be met at the door by an anxious Mr Whiting.

"I don't know what's going on tonight," he greeted her. "But Luke was troubled about you. He said if you didn't come home soon I should set out to search for you."

"Where is he?" she broke in.

"Gone — he left half an hour ago."

"Gone! Oh no! Where did he go?"

The merchant shook his head.

"I don't know. Or rather, I do. He left word that if you wanted to come after him you'd find him at the 'Anchor' at Gravesend until midday tomorrow —

156

after that he'll be at sea. That's all he said."

Gravesend! She could set out in pursuit; but it might take hours to find him — and then she had to persuade him to tell her what he knew — and only then set out to find the Earl. There was no time. She stood in silent anguish, praying for some solution to come to her.

In the end she knew there was only one way open to her, and that an almost hopeless one. She must take the Dover road and embark on the impossible task of searching miles of countryside for one ruined farmhouse, in the vain hope that she might reach it before her husband's murderers.

She told Mr Whiting only that she must go out, and might not be back for a day or two. After that she would let him know her plans. Lastly she apologised for imposing on him, but begged him to lend her a sturdy horse. She had money, she said, and would pay whatever seemed a fair hire.

He would take no money, but lent the horse and offered to send a servant with her, an offer she declined: her mission was too secret for that. But she thanked him warmly, took her cloak and some money and set out in the warm darkness through the empty streets, the hooves clattering loudly on the cobbles.

By the time she had crossed the river and reached the countryside to the south the sky had already paled a little. It would very soon be daylight. The birds were beginning to stir in the trees lining the road. She had a long way to go, and time was passing with terrifying speed.

At least Mr Whiting had been generous with the horse. He was not a high-spirited animal, but what he lacked in speed he more than made up for in strength and stamina, and that mattered far more. She had no time to pause for rest or food.

She did halt once or twice as the day passed, but

only to ask at inn or tavern if a rider answering the Earl's description had come that way yesterday. When she heard at Rochester that he had indeed called there to eat yesterday afternoon she rode on with renewed vigour, fired by something that was not quite hope.

She was close to exhaustion when she reached Canterbury as dusk fell, and by now her horse was little better. In her weary state despair crept over her spirit. I was foolish, she thought, even to suppose for a moment that I had a chance of finding Benedict in time. Better rather to have stayed at home and prayed for his safety.

But she knew she could have done nothing else than this, and she must go on. It was then, halting for the food and rest she knew she must have both for the horse and for herself, that she learnt that the Earl had spent last night in the best inn at Canterbury. He came there quite often, they told her. It was said there was a lady at some village east of the Dover road. Once they had been seen together just outside Canterbury.

Olivia's heart gave a great leap of delight, and then twisted again with a sharp pang which she did not pause to examine. A lady! Had Luke been wrong after all? Was it only a lady that brought him here, and was all the talk of intrigue with France and an agent in a ruined farmhouse a figment of Luke's imagination? Somehow the lady was more in keeping with what she had once believed the Earl's character to be than Luke's tale of fanaticism and treachery. Or was the lady simply an invention, a useful cover — as she herself was — for her husband's secret and deadly activities?

Olivia gave herself a little shake. It did not matter which was true, for the one certain thing was that the Earl himself was in terrible danger. There was no time to lose.

Refreshed a little, her weariness forgotten, Olivia set out half an hour later on a fresh horse. The field had been narrowed a little. The lady came from a village east of the Dover road, they had said. That might not be a clue at all to the location of the farmhouse, but she could not search everywhere and it would have to do.

It would have been difficult enough to find a ruined farmhouse in this unknown countryside in daylight. But now it was almost dark, and Olivia soon realised that, alone, her task was hopeless. Only the lights of villages and inhabited farmhouses gave her any guidance through the rutted lanes, and without local knowledge she would never succeed. She knocked at the first door she reached to ask for help, but the people were suspicious and turned her away. She was close to tears by the time she found an inn, but she swallowed them with fierce determination and asked the landlord if he knew of a deserted farmhouse in the district.

He knew of two. One, two miles away, had been empty for years — since the war, he believed — and was almost a ruin and said to be haunted. The other, a mile in the other direction, had been empty since last year. The owners, with relations in London, had gone down one by one with the plague. They were no sooner dead than the house was looted by their neighbours and stripped of all it contained. Some said that house was haunted now too.

Luke had told Olivia the farmhouse was ruined. She would go to the further one in the hope that it might be what she was seeking. She refused the landlord's offer of a guide — it would not help to involve anyone else in this affair — but accepted a lantern, and carefully memorised the man's meticulous directions.

The two miles in the darkness lit only dimly by the swaying lantern seemed interminable to Olivia.

159

The landlord's directions had been good, using every possible landmark — even a twisted tree or a gate post — to guide her; but even so Olivia was often forced to dismount and look about her in bank and hedgerow before she could be sure of the way. She came at last to a crossroads which she had been told was close to the ruin, and there paused again to make sure she was not mistaken. It was then that she heard, coming steadily towards her along the road from the left, the sound of approaching hooves.

Quickly she extinguished the lantern and led her horse into the trees beside the road. Her heart was beating so loudly that it almost shut out the sound of the hooves. She strained her ears to miss nothing.

There was more than one horse. Benedict and his servant? If so, then her search was over, successful beyond her wildest hopes.

The horses came nearer, drew level, halted just out of sight behind a bush. They had a lantern, too, for its light spread beyond them on the road, bobbing from side to side. Slowly, they moved into sight; two men walking in front with the lantern, examining the road to see which way to take, and two behind leading the horses. None of them was tall or fair or known to her in any way.

Olivia pressed her hand to her mouth to suppress the involuntary gasp of dismay. Luke's friends — that was who they must be. And they had almost reached their goal. Was the Earl already there, waiting unsuspecting in the darkness? Or would they reach there before him, and lie hidden until he came? Whatever happened, he would have no defence against a surprise attack by four men at dead of night, even if he still had a servant with him. And on such a secret mission he might well be alone.

No defence, unless she could warn him first. She must reach the farmhouse and find out if he was there. And reach it at once, before these men did so.

She knew now which road led from here to the farmhouse. The men were still discussing the matter. It gave her a moment or two, perhaps just long enough —

Olivia let go of her horse's bridle and gave him a vigorous slap on the flank. With a snort of astonishment he crashed through the undergrowth and then onto the road behind the men. They turned and exclaimed and began to search the trees at the point where he had emerged. The diversion gave Olivia the opportunity she needed. As fast and as quietly as she could she ran across the road which had brought her here, through the trees at the further side and along the track beyond, which twisted its way under the faint moonlight towards the clearing where the ruined farmhouse stood.

She could only just make out its shape, a denser black in the darkness, and she had not brought the lantern with her. There was no light that she could see among the ruins.

The roof had fallen in, and the walls, never high, had crumbled in places to a heap of rubble. But on the far side an outbuilding of some kind was still intact, and through a small square opening in the wall a dim light shone. Olivia ran towards it, and very slowly, holding her breath, edged near enough to see in.

He was there, seated patiently on a rough stool, a dark cloak covering his finery, his fair head resting on the wall behind him. A single candle flame lit his face, its closed lids, the straight nose and the fine mouth. Olivia's stomach gave a lurch which had nothing to do with fear or imminent danger.

And then a hand grasped her arm, another slapped across her mouth, and she was dragged back from the window. She tried to scream, but only a muffled sound emerged, and she kicked and struggled wildly. But whoever held her was very strong, and very

161

determined. He dragged her with him, relentlessly, and she had no choice but to go.

He took her, not back into the concealment of the trees, but round and into the rough unplastered room where Benedict sat, and there in the candle-light turned her to face her husband. For a moment Olivia was aware only of his face, the eyes opening wide and blue with amazement, the sudden dangerous alertness, as of some jungle animal.

"Found her outside, my lord —" her captor began to explain; and then broke off with a cry as she bit into his palm. Somehow she must give her warning, before it was too late.

But it was already too late. With a crash as the worn timbers splintered the door flew open, and the four men tumbled in. Olivia turned sharply in time to see that they had at the least a gun and three swords between them; and then she was thrust aside. She fell awkwardly, her head striking the wall. There was a moment of bright light and searing pain, and then oblivion.

She must have come round almost at once, for it was not over yet. Near her a man lay still on the ground, but the pain in her head was too great for her to look closely at him. She was confusedly aware of the light catching the shining length of a sword blade, and of the dark shapes of men in desperate combat. The Earl's fair hair gleamed briefly: so he was still fighting; but it could not be for long.

Despairingly, not wanting to see the end, she closed her eyes again. And as she did so a black outline on the straw near her head caught her attention: a pistol, perhaps knocked from the hand of one of them as he came in, and left there because he could not with safety retrieve it. Olivia knew about guns: her father had taught her, long ago. She reached out an unsteady hand and pulled it towards her. And then, very slowly, her eyes shut against the throbbing in her head, she drew herself up to sit with her back against the wall.

Now, when she looked again, she could see how close-pressed the Earl was. It was one of Luke's friends who lay near her, for Benedict's servant fought at his side, a long knife in his hand. They were more evenly matched than at first, and the Earl fought with breathtaking dexterity, but he was hard-pressed with three swords moving always closer inside the length of his shining blade. Olivia examined the pistol, checking that it was loaded, and levelled it carefully, as steadily and accurately as a headache and trembling hands would allow. And then she fired.

The explosion of sound shook the little building, and the man nearest to her husband fell with a groan to the ground. She had aimed at his sword arm, but she feared she had hurt him more than that.

For an instant the two other men paused, and looked round; and it gave Benedict the chance he needed. As swordsmen they were no match for him, and very soon he and his man had them driven back against the far wall, their weapons thrown to the floor. Once they were bound and the servant standing guard over them, the Earl turned his attention to his wife. Olivia watched him come, her eyes very dark in her white face. She was too shaken and exhausted to smile. And when he spoke, breathless from recent exertion, she knew she had no reason to smile.

"So you missed!" he sneered. "You should take some lessons in shooting before you try your hand with a pistol again. Only I shall be forewarned another time, and know what to expect from you. How does it feel to shoot one of your own friends?" He bent down and picked up the pistol from where she had let it fall, and then he loaded it and passed it to his servant.

"Take those two with you and find their horses. Send someone from the first inn you reach to pick up these others — I'll think up some story to account for them. I'll see you in Canterbury."

"And the woman?" That was the first certain indication Olivia had that the man had never seen her before: it gave her a very slight feeling of relief.

"I'll bring her along," said the Earl. "It will be my pleasure." Even during that last dreadful quarrel he had not spoken with such venom. Olivia shivered, and closed her eyes against the contemptuous anger of his face.

"I wanted to warn you," she murmured faintly. The noise of the servant prodding the two prisoners before him with his pistol as they left the hut destroyed what little chance there was that Benedict would hear her.

She realised that he must now be dragging the two motionless bodies to one side of the room, perhaps so that he could more easily keep an eye on them. One of the men groaned as he was moved. Olivia opened her eyes and saw that it was the one she had shot.

"He's not dead then!" Her quiet relieved exclamation escaped from her before she could think of how it would sound to her husband. She was glad simply that she had not been guilty of murder, but to the Earl it would only seem to confirm her guilt, and her friendship with the men who had sought his death. He lodged the wounded man briskly but not unkindly against the wall, and then turned again to look at her.

"No, he's not dead. Just as well, isn't it? Your other friends might not want to speak to you again if he were. As it is, he'll live, if we can get attention to him soon."

"They're not my friends!" she cried out. "I've never seen any of them before tonight."

He raised a sceptical eyebrow.

"Indeed? A very odd coincidence that you should arrive exactly as they did in a place so isolated as this. As it is I am astonished that anyone should know I

164

was here at all — apart from those who are meant to know, that is."

Perhaps he was referring to the lady they had spoken of in Canterbury. Olivia wondered idly what had become of her, and what she would say if she were faced with this scene on her arrival. On the other hand, it was probable that there was no lady involved at all, only the agent Luke had mentioned. It was all too confusing for Olivia's weary brain. She could barely find the will or the energy even to defend herself against the Earl's suspicions.

"I don't know them," she reasserted, stubbornly but without force. "I have never met them before. I came to warn you. I found out they were on their way —"

He smiled derisively.

"You had never met them, yet you knew they were on their way? I find that fascinating. You must have extraordinary supernatural powers. Or are they part of a much larger conspiracy? Do enlighten me, my lady Countess!"

She could not bear to meet his gaze, so full was it of a hard and relentless light. She felt cold and hopeless, as if everything had crumbled to ashes about her. Yet he was alive, and that was what she had wanted above all.

"Luke told me," she said slowly. "He knew about it all. He's gone now, overseas."

"Ah yes, your very dear friend! I guessed you'd run to him. You were to join him later, I suppose, conveniently freed by my death to be his wife? But clearly you could not resist the prospect of being present at the kill. I am sorry to disappoint you —"

His eyes ran over her, bright and deadly like those of a snake; when he spoke again he seemed to spit the words at her: "And to think I loved you once!"

She drew in her breath, sharply, as if in pain — no, not 'as if', for the pain was real, a cruel piercing thrust like a knife twisting in her heart. It took all power of speech from her, all clarity of thought. She knew only that there had been no anguish like this in all her life before. 'Let it end!' something cried inside her. 'Let it not be happening! Let me wake — or die — for this is more than I can bear!'

But it did not end. Instead the bitter outpouring went on, relentless, full of hatred.

"Dear God, I was blind — more blind than I knew! It suited you to be my wife, with an eye on all my secrets — it suited Luke, too — a nice pair of spies! I was not far wrong when I guessed you planned sedition together in bed. Only you added murder to that. You looked forward to being a widow, didn't you — that would bring you Spensley and Luke, all the heart could desire? But be sure of one thing, my lady wife, I shall make very certain that you have neither, ever again. You will never see Spensley again; and you will not go to Luke, wherever he is —"

He broke off suddenly, his attention caught even in his mood of bitter anger by the sound of an approaching horse. Olivia sat shivering, not caring what might happen next, not even able to feel a sense of relief that he was silent at last.

Outside the hoofbeats ceased, and there was a moment of quiet. And then someone came through the dark jagged opening of the doorway into the candlelight.

No burly inn servant took shape there, no dark-cloaked agent, no man at all; but a woman. She was tall and graceful and golden-haired, and Olivia recognised her at once. She had seen this woman last at Spensley, coming with the men to one of those long secret conferences from which she was so grimly excluded. So the lady he came here to meet was no mistress, but a fellow conspirator; and what Luke had said must be true in every respect. It was as if the last piece of the puzzle fell into place.

The woman paused in the doorway, and her eyes went from the Earl to Olivia and back again, and then to the two still figures on the floor. Then she said quickly: "What's happened? Who are these?"

"I have had visitors," said the Earl. "I will explain some other time. For now, let me have the letter, and then go home. You have it with you, of course?"

She nodded, and pulled a folded paper, heavily sealed, from beneath her cloak, and held it out to him. He took it, and concealed it in his doublet, and then she murmured 'goodnight' and disappeared into the darkness.

Olivia watched in weary misery until they were alone again, and then she said heavily: "So it was all true, what Luke said — I had hoped . . ."

The Earl shot her one hostile glance.

"I know what you hoped. Spare me the explanations."

A small spark of anger revived in her.

"Why will you not believe me? I came to warn you."

"I am sick of hearing you beg me to believe you. I've believed you once too often. I should have had more sense than to trust you for one single moment. 'We are like brother and sister,' you said — or was it Luke who said it? It makes no difference, for there was never a grain of truth in it, was there?"

She could not find the strength to try and explain. She said only, "I'm not in league with Luke. There is nothing between us, and I do not want there to be." But she knew it was hopeless. She knew it even without looking up at his stony expression, the cold mouth and colder eyes.

Soon afterwards the men arrived from the inn with a cart. The Earl ordered them to lift the two bodies onto the vehicle, instructing them to send the wounded man on to London as soon as he was well enough. Then he turned to Olivia.

"Get to your feet," he said curtly. His pistol at

167

her waist, he prodded her out into the clearing where his horse, and those of the two fallen men, were waiting; and there he commanded her brusquely to mount, keeping the reins in his own hand. Then they set out in the growing daylight, riding slowly side by side, in a grotesque companionship.

She was so tired that it took an enormous effort of will to sit upright in the saddle. She felt cold, too, despite the warmth of the night, and very sick, though she had eaten nothing for many hours. She did not think she would ever want to eat again. More than once she found her lids closing, weighted with weariness, and her head falling forward with a jerk. Twice she knew she had for a few moments been fully asleep.

They halted soon in an inn yard, and she was aware, dimly, that her husband had hired a coach, and that somehow she had dismounted and found herself seated in it, with the Earl at a chilly distance on the far side. She had a painful recollection of other journeys: the very first, when his attentiveness had been so unwelcome; the second, on their wedding day, when some sure instinct had told him the comfort she needed. "I loved you once," he had said tonight. Was that how he had been able to understand her so well?

But that way lay the pain from which for the moment weariness shielded her. She did not want to probe the wound and set it throbbing again in all its agonising intensity. Instead, she turned her head a little so that she could see the Earl's profile, outlined in perfect silhouette against the grey paleness of the window.

"What do you mean to do now?" she asked tonelessly. He looked round, though it was not light enough yet inside the coach for her to read his expression. That, she thought, was just as well, for she had seen too much of its hatred and bitterness in the past hours.

"With you, you mean? Oh, never fear, you will be spared the fate you deserve. Your friends will be brought to justice, but you are still — God help us! — my wife. I shall take you to your brother's house. They will be glad enough to keep you there in seclusion — they won't want to broadcast our estrangement to the world; and I shall make you a fair allowance. You will want for nothing. Except Luke, of course. I have no intention of freeing you — I take my vows seriously, if you do not. But clearly any life together is impossible now. It's a pity I didn't realise it was never possible; but there we are. Spensley will have to do without an heir."

Olivia bent her head, fighting back the sudden rush of tears. Relentlessly, the Earl went on:

"You need not try and run to Luke. Your brother will have strict instructions to keep you under constant observation. After this escapade you must not be trusted again. Simply be thankful you get off so lightly."

She did not make any further attempt to protest her innocence: she knew it was hopeless, as everything was hopeless. She faced a future without light, without joy, without anything but constant remorse and grief and pain.

When the coach drew to a halt late that evening in the familiar street she had last seen silenced by the plague, she thought: 'I should have stayed here. Better far to have died of the plague, than this.'

ELEVEN

A week in her brother's house told Olivia many things. The first, and most obvious, was that her marriage had already brought them prosperity. Fashionable courtiers had begun to place their orders with Henry, and the effects of this new patronage were clear in the new furnishings, the pictures and musical instruments, the children's tutor, the extra servants, Celia's fine new clothes. Having done so well from her marriage, Henry and Celia were not pleased that it appeared to have come to an end so soon; but at least that ensured that they did not make the estrangement a subject for gossip. And the Earl paid them well for their guardianship of his wife.

The children, on the other hand, were glad to see her again. But even there it was not as it had been. Paulina was already showing signs of her mother's boldness, and the coy self-consciousness was unattractive in one so young. Soon, Olivia thought sadly, the other children too would be tainted by the atmosphere of the house. But she, who had so stupidly ruined her own life, was in no position to influence them for good.

With time to think and even, alone in her small room high under the roof, some intervals of time to herself, Olivia could look back with chilling clarity over the past months. She could see now how, time and again, she had taken a wrong step, this way or that, blind to her own feelings, blind to what could have been hers.

'I loved you once.' From his angry bitter outpouring in the ruined farmhouse Olivia had learned the truth at last. The hurt in his voice and in his eyes had told her as clearly as any words that Benedict had married her for one reason only: because he loved her. That, if she had only seen it, had been why he had been so kind and courteous and attentive in the early days of their marriage, shyly wooing her so that she might one day come to love him in return. That explained too his jealousy of her, for he had feared to lose her to someone else before he had won her for himself. He knew he could arouse her passion; but he wanted her heart.

Now, too late, when he no longer cared, he held it unknowingly in his hands, and there was nothing she could do to free it from its imprisonment. She loved him, and because she had not realised it until now she must live with the bitter knowledge that she had lost him for ever. How blind she had been to think that it was Luke she had loved! Her affection for him had been always simply the warm friendship she had claimed it to be, and nothing else. Had he not come back when she was still unsure of herself, still doubting the wisdom of the marriage she had made, she would have known at once that she did not want to marry him, and never would have done. If only, then, she had known that her husband had loved her!

She thought very little of the plot in which the Earl was involved. She did not doubt that it existed, and she supposed that Luke was right, and that it posed a real threat to the freedom they held dear. But it seemed somehow unreal and unimportant set against the solid horrible fact of her ruined marriage. 'If only —' she found herself thinking so often that first week in London; and it led on always to that deadly phrase 'too late'. There was no way back.

And then on a hot Saturday night at the beginning of September, one week after her return, a sudden stunning realisation changed everything.

Henry and Celia had gathered their friends for a

supper party. Olivia knew their parties of old, and she had never liked them. She had hoped that her difficult position might exclude her from the company, but Henry merely told her she must be there, so that he could keep an eye on her, though she could, he said, sit in a corner all night if she wished. That at least was better than being forced to take part. But as the drinking grew deeper, and the dancing wilder, and couples retired to fondle one another away from the brightest lights, she found it less and less bearable to be a solitary onlooker. She longed to go to bed, or into the garden, away from the heat and the noise and the smell of over-perfumed, underwashed bodies; and the too close attentions of a drunken neighbour, undeterred by the severely Puritan cap and gown in which she had dressed this evening.

What it was that suddenly brought the knowledge home to her she did not know, but it must have been nearly midnight when all at once she knew with complete certainty that she was pregnant. It struck through her misery and disgust like a shaft of light. So that last night of love had not been the end — it was not all over! She had lost the love of the man with whom she longed above all to pass the rest of her life; but she was carrying his child.

Wonderingly, she laid her hand over her flat stomach, and thought of the new life growing in there. New life, new hope, new love: she was no longer alone.

But there were too many people here, and she longed for the party to end so that she could have time to herself, to think and to plan. It seemed hours before the last guests had gone, rolling noisy and drunken down the stairs to stagger the few doors to their own homes or stumble into a waiting coach. Olivia began half-heartedly to gather up some of the debris of the evening — spilled wine glasses, sweet-meats squashed into the floor — while Henry barred the front door and came yawning up the stairs to where Celia slumped sleepily in a chair.

"It must be close on two o'clock," he said. "I'm going to bed." Celia pulled herself to her feet, swaying a little.

"I think I shall go and walk in the garden for a little while," Olivia announced quietly. She waited for Henry's protest, but none came. He was too drunk to care very much what she did, and in any case the garden did not provide any easy means of escape, had she been looking for one.

"We'll not wait up," was all he said. "Be sure and bar the door when you come in."

It was quiet in the garden, blissfully quiet, with a pleasant breeze cooling the air. Olivia sank onto a wooden bench and closed her eyes and allowed the tranquillity of the moonlit evening to creep into her tired body.

'I am going to have a child,' she thought. 'I know I am going to have a child. Benedict's child, and mine.' Whatever happened, she would cherish this new life growing within her, looking forward to the day when it would lie in her arms, a baby she could touch and see and love.

"Spensley will have to do without an heir," her husband had said in that tone of bitter acceptance. But he had been wrong, for the flame of their passion had already kindled the little spark of life which would give Spensley its heir.

Only he must never know.

That certainty struck Olivia like a blight to her new happiness. She saw only too well what would happen if she told him of the child. Everything was over between them, he had made that plain. But the child was his as much as hers, heir to a title and to the great estates which went with it. No father in the Earl's position would dream of turning his back on that fact. He would insist that the child was raised and educated

173

in a manner appropriate to its place in society — at Spensley, most likely. He would, almost certainly, demand that his heir should be brought up in his own faith. And he would without any doubt at all exclude from any possibility of influence on the child the wife who had so disastrously failed him. She was disgraced and put aside: she could not hope to be allowed to play any part in caring for her own child.

So he must not know. And that meant that Henry and Celia must not know either, for they would certainly regard it as their duty to inform him once her condition was obvious.

Long before that time she must leave this house, escape to some safe retreat where the child could be born in secret and raised away from any fear of his discovery.

Restless, troubled, Olivia rose to her feet and wandered miserably about the garden, trying to think of some other way out. It was the cruellest fate of all, to know she must keep from the man she loved the knowledge that she was carrying their child. If only — if only she had known of this before she left Spensley, and could have told him then. Perhaps, even in the midst of that terrible quarrel, it would have been enough to bring them together, to save their marriage before it was too late.

But thinking like that only made the pain more unbearable. She must learn to face the future, to scheme and plan for herself and her child, for their life together. That they should have a life together was all that mattered to her now. She pressed her hands to her face and tried to clear her mind of anything but the cool powers of reasoning which she would need so much.

It was then that she became aware that the garden was no longer the quiet haven she had thought it. Into her troubled mind came new, strange, unfamiliar sounds. Shouting, a scream, running feet, and a sharp crackling – a noise like that of a fire burning in a hearth, only magnified many times.

With a start she drew her hands from her eyes. There, to the east, just a short way off, the sky was red. Not distantly red, with the first light of dawn, but luridly, horribly red, with flames licking upwards into the night sky, tipped with black smoke against the stars. As she watched a sudden explosive sound burst out and more flames shot up to join the others. A growing wall of flame danced hideously above the rooftops. Something was on fire. And something very near to where she sat, no more than two or three streets away.

Olivia jumped to her feet and ran indoors, all her own anxieties put aside. Remembering Henry's instructions she barred the door behind her; and then turned to find that Jane had entered the kitchen.

"Have you seen it?" asked the maid. She looked pale and a little frightened, shivering in her shift, though the night was not cold.

"The fire? Yes, I saw it. It's very near – and after so long without rain –"

Jane nodded at the implication of Olivia's remark. She slept with the other servants in a room beside Olivia's own high under the eaves, commanding a good view over the rooftops.

"I was lying there wakeful, and the next thing I knew the sky was all red, and there was the sound of shouting, and crackling flames."

"Do you think we should wake them all?"

Jane frowned.

"Which way's the wind blowing tonight?"

Olivia pondered the question for a moment, and then replied: "From the east, I think."

"Then it'll blow this way. There's nothing but wood and plaster between us and that fire. And it's spreading fast – I could see that much from above. Shall I go and see if I can find out what's happening?"

175

Olivia nodded gratefully. "But take care," she added.

Jane was not gone very long. She came back at a run, and gasped out: "They're leaving the houses all around us. The fire started in Pudding Lane — at Mr Farriner's bakery — and it's already reached Fish Street. It has a firm hold, and no one's lifting a finger to stop it."

"Then I'll go and wake my brother."

It was easier said than done. Both Henry and his wife had drunk too much tonight to be woken easily. They lay on their backs snoring gently and rhythmically, and it was a long time before Olivia's frantic shaking stirred her half-brother to open reluctant and bleary eyes. When he saw who bent over him he gave a groan and turned away from her onto his side.

Olivia dragged at his shoulder.

"Henry!" she cried urgently, no longer troubling to whisper. "Wake up! There's a fire!"

After more shaking her words at last penetrated his drink-sodden brain, and he leaned up on one elbow, yawning.

"What's that? A fire? Is the house alight?" Already Celia had reached for a gown and was climbing from the bed at its far side.

"Not yet," said Olivia. "But it's close — two streets away perhaps — and coming this way. I think we should be ready."

Celia sank back on the pillows, scowling.

"Don't be foolish, Olivia. You should have waited until it was nearer than that before waking us. Very likely it'll not spread so far."

"Come and see for yourself," Olivia invited, gesturing towards the window.

Grumbling volubly, Henry crossed the room, Celia following him. Olivia herself was alarmed to see how much the fire had spread since she had watched it from the garden. Even as they stood there the flames

176

moved explosively one leaping step nearer, flakes of burning debris scattering over the rooftops towards them. It would take one such spark on timbers dry as tinder after the long drought, and the whole street about them would be consumed. Celia gave a soft cry.

"We must gather the valuables together — find a cart — there's no time to be lost. We can take shelter somewhere until the flames die down."

Olivia left them dressing and went to rouse the servants and wake and dress the children. She did not want to frighten them, but she had somehow to stir them from sleep, to urge them to hurry, drowsy as they were.

"There's a house on fire a little way away," she told them matter-of-factly. "So we're going to find somewhere a bit further off where we can spend the night."

Fortunately the children were more awestruck and excited than frightened as they glimpsed the red sky from the landing window and hurried down into the street clutching their most-loved toys.

There Henry was supervising the loading of a cart with his best silver, the musical instruments, the most valuable wine from his store, Celia's favourite gowns and what jewellery she possessed. The street was noisy with their neighbours doing the same, shouting, running, stumbling in grey faced panic.

At last they were ready. The cart set out rumbling along the street, Henry and Celia walking behind to make sure nothing fell from it — or was stolen — on the way. Olivia followed with the children, and those of the servants who were not urging on the frightened carthorse.

"Some are going to the churches for safety," Jane told them. But a neighbour called: "St Magnus' church is alight already — you want to get right away." And Henry nodded his agreement.

"We'll walk as far as we can — find an open space

with no houses about it — it's a fine dry night and we'll take no harm — it'll soon be morning in any case."

They trudged on through streets beginning to fill as if it were daytime. Once beyond reach of the horrible sounds of the fire — though whenever they turned to look the sky glowed more evilly red than ever — they slowed their pace a little, and Henry began to look about him for a suitable place in which his household might camp. The first light of dawn was just paling the sky beyond the leaping flames when he found it — a wide grassy space set aside in happier times for the playing of bowls. Now several families were already vying for the security it offered.

Henry led the way resolutely to its furthest side, drove off a poor pinched-looking woman and two children who had no goods to carry with them, and ordered the servants to halt the cart as far from the fire's reach as possible. And then they settled on the grass to rest as best they could.

Though there was little rest for any of them while the sky glowed so fiercely. They watched in fascination as the fire spread to the north and the south and came steadily, surely, nearer, throwing up showers of deadly sparks, exploding now and then to shoot a great new wall of flame against the greying sky. It was fascinating, and yet utterly horrible.

"I've seen many a fire in this city," observed one of Henry's elderly servants, "but never one to spread so fast."

"Do you think it was started on purpose?" the cook asked.

"Easy enough for a fire to start by chance in a bakery," Jane pointed out sensibly. "And it's been so dry this summer."

"First the plague, then this!" murmured the cook.

Suddenly Celia's voice broke into the desultory talk in an anguished wail.

"My little dog — my Punchinello — he's not here!"

They turned to gaze at her as her voice rose higher and higher, close to screaming pitch. "My Punchinello, my darling little Punchinello — he'll be burned — oh, Henry, what can I do?"

Henry patted her shoulder, totally without effect, and muttered something about "Very likely he'll not feel much." It was not the wisest reply. Celia gave a shriek of horror, and cried out:

"Someone must go back for him now, at once. We can't leave him to burn!" Faces gazed blankly back at her. No one moved or spoke. The fire was close enough now for them to hear the roar and crackle of the flames above the voices of the fugitives. "Jane, you go!" commanded Celia frantically. "Or you, John, you're a man — you go."

Old John opened his mouth to protest, but no sound emerged. As if against his will his eyes travelled to the flames and lingered there.

"We'll have to move on again soon," observed the cook, as if hoping to divert his mistress's attention. But as a tactic it failed dismally.

"John, you must go — I order you to go! Henry, tell him!" Henry stirred uneasily.

"You'd better go," he advised the old man. John was about to pull himself to his feet when Olivia broke in.

"No," she said severely. "John's an old man — we've walked a long way already, and he can't move quickly. It's not fair to ask him to risk his life for a dog." And as Celia opened her mouth indignantly she went on: "I'll go." But she did not allow Celia to express her effusive thanks. "I'll not risk my life either," she warned. "If it's safe I'll search the house for your dog. But I'm not going anywhere near if it's alight. Henry's right, I'm sure, that he'd not suffer much."

"Don't talk — go! And" — as Olivia began to hurry away from them — "bring my red velvet gown as well

179

— I forgot it in the rush."

Olivia resisted the temptation to turn back with a cutting retort, and moved faster. She would not risk her life or her health for the dog, but she would not wish it to suffer if there was any way of saving it. On the other hand she had no intention at all of rescuing the velvet gown.

The throng in the streets was terrible now, and it was all she could do to push her way inch by slow inch against its relentless flow. Once, a man caught at her sleeve, and called out: "Don't go that way, wench. You'll burn!" But she ignored him and thrust on into the crowd.

As she came nearer to the edge of the fire sparks blew fitfully in her face and the heat scorched her even some way off. Here, most of the people had already fled, though some waited until the flames had almost engulfed their homes before they ran for safety into the street. At last, Olivia turned a corner and came face to face with the fire, a fierce impenetrable barrier across her path.

There was no hope that way. She stood gazing about her trying to see where she was, and if there was any other way to approach Henry's house, though she was sure already that the dog must be past saving. Then all at once the flames engulfed the house beside which she stood, leaping through it with a roar and a scorching wind which almost sucked her into its heart. She jumped aside just in time before the flames could catch the light fabric of her gown.

There was nothing for it now but to retrace her steps. Out in the quieter streets in the great sinister shadow of the fire she paused to look around. She was not yet ready to give up altogether. The fire was at its worst, she noticed, alongside the river — she had heard them say that London Bridge had already caught — but to the north she might still find a way.

She had little hope that Henry's house would have escaped, but while there was a chance she would take it.

Stung by sparks, scorched by the heat, soiled by the charred fragments which hung in the air, she plodded on through emptying streets, threading a path through little knots of fugitives, steadily working her way north and then turning south again when she knew she had come level with her own street. To the west was a horrible desolation, flames flickering and smouldering amongst blackened ruins which had once been homes, over scorched gardens in which no flower or tree remained. At least — thank God — there was no obvious sign that any human lives had been lost, though she could not be sure of that.

By some strange freak in the direction of the wind their own street still stood, on the very edge of the fire. But she was only just in time. The flames were already moving inexorably towards her as she made her way over cobbles strewn with goods lost or thrown away in flight. As she reached Henry's front door the neighbouring house fell with a roar and a crackle and a crashing of timbers. Not pausing to think, she pushed open the door and ran inside.

"Punchinello!" she called, glancing frantically about her as she ran. "Punchinello! Come on now — it's all right — you'll be safe now!" But not for long, she thought. In a moment this house too would be swallowed up, and if she did not find the dog in time she would be consumed with everything else. She ran up the stairs, calling and calling, but no answering yap met her ears, no sound but the roar of the flames next door.

Her heart beating faster she searched each room one by one, under beds, behind curtains, in every corner, but there was no sign of the dog. She ran down the stairs again, along the passage, into the kitchen.

And there she found him, cowering in terror by the dying embers of the fire as the greater flames outside licked their way towards the window, reddening the sky as if a great wound bled into it. Olivia seized the trembling creature in her arms and fled towards the open front door. And at that moment the flames engulfed the whole of the front of the house, shooting up before her in a sheet of ghastly crimson. Olivia screamed.

The dog whined and struggled in her arms, and she clutched him tighter and backed away down the passage. Already as she ran under them the stairs caught fire. One-handed, she wrenched at the bar which held the kitchen door closed, cursing her own care which had secured it so firmly before the dawn.

It came open at last and she ran into the garden. She could not see the wall which separated the garden next door from their own. It was hidden in flame and smoke, and at the end of the garden another house was burning too. Soon the fire would reach the other side and she would be cut off from any hope of escape. There was a wall, but it was high, and she had the dog in her arms to hamper her.

She buried her face momentarily in the dog's fur and prayed desperately, wordlessly, for a miracle.

And against all the odds a voice reached her, calling her name.

"Olivia!"

She looked up, and the tall figure of her husband sprang down from the wall which the fire had not yet reached.

TWELVE

He wasted no time in talk, but seized her about the waist and flung her up to the top of the wall. One-handed, she hung on but could not pull herself the last few inches. Cursing the dog he grasped one of her legs and edged it over the top, and she perched there, precariously, swaying a little.

"Is there anyone else in there?" he demanded, nodding towards the house. She shook her head, thinking at the same time that if there had been they would have been past help by now in any case, for the kitchen had gone too. The heat shrivelled the plants at the foot of the wall.

The Earl dragged himself up the wall and jumped down at the far side, pausing there to reach up to her.

"Jump!" he commanded. She dropped into his arms, and the dog yelped as it was half-crushed between them. "Can't you let that thing go?"

"No! — I came all this way back for him."

He gave her an exasperated glance, but said no more, grasping her arm and leading her across their neighbour's garden. The flames were already licking about the timbers of the building.

Between this house and the next was a narrow entry. Benedict dragged Olivia towards it. It was their one way of escape, but if the house went up before they were safely through they would go with it. Olivia followed blindly, clutching the dog, her mind one wordless prayer.

They made it, emerging into the street just as the flames reached the entry, paused for a brief moment and then shot across it as if no man-made barrier

183

could keep them at bay. The Earl set out at a run along the as yet unburned part of the street pulling Olivia with him as the great wall of fire followed them, licking and roaring its way at either side, nearer and nearer to where they ran.

Olivia felt dizzy and breathless with fear and exhaustion, but some willpower kept her going, her legs moving mechanically, running, running a few paces behind her rescuer. He did not slow his pace or speak until the flames were well behind them and they had reached the thronged streets to the north of the fire which she had passed earlier this morning. And here at last, he halted and turned to look at her.

"We mustn't stay here — it's moving fast. I have a boat on the river."

"But the others!" gasped Olivia when she found her voice at last. "I must go back to them. They were over near St Paul's."

"Then they'll have moved on again. The fire's taken hold not far from there — and may even be there already by now. You'll not find them again today. I'll take you to safety now, and we'll look for them when you've rested, if that's what you wish."

Olivia was too weary to argue. All about her people were gathering to watch the fire, to shake their heads over it and discuss its progress with excited horror. Olivia was glad to allow herself to be led away from their clamour.

Benedict took her at a less exhausting pace towards the east, beyond the range of the fire, and then through narrow streets to the river's edge, where his boat waited, the waterman ready to leave at his command. He handed her in, the boat rocking gently as she stepped into it. And then he jumped in after her, and urged her to sit down. Olivia lay wearily back on the velvet cushions, the dog clasped in her arms, and closed her eyes. She was dimly aware of her husband stretching out beside her, and ordering the boatman to take them home. Smoothly the boat moved out from the shore.

She did not stir for a long time. Too much had happened tonight for her to be able yet to take it in. She only knew she was safe, and that somehow, by some miracle too great to comprehend, it was Benedict who had saved her and who sat now at her side. After a moment or two she felt his arm slide about her shoulder, drawing her against him. Later, she would dare to find out if indeed the miracle was greater even than she dared to hope. For now she was thankful only to rest.

The boat steered a course as far as possible from the northern bank of the river, and as it made its way towards London Bridge the whole terrible extent of the fire could be seen. It would have been almost magnificent, that red glowing sky lit with sparks, darkened with smoke, spreading now from near where it had first taken hold almost to St Paul's cathedral, prominent on its hill. Only, it was Henry's house that was burning, and those of a thousand others like him, and with their homes, for the most part, went all their belongings and their livelihoods. Olivia shuddered.

"It moves so fast!" she murmured.

"Yes," agreed the Earl. "The wind's behind it, and all the wood so dry —" His hold tightened about her as if he was remembering how nearly she had perished in those same fast-moving flames.

The boat approached London Bridge, with its stone arches spanning the river, and its northern end fiercely ablaze. But the boatman steered the craft neatly beneath the southernmost arch, the faces of his passengers catching the red light as they emerged to where the fire now raged most furiously.

Here, even in the river, burning timbers fell and

185

hissed flaming for long seconds until the water extinguished them at last. Everywhere boats pushed out from the fiery shoreline laden with goods, desperately seeking safety. It was the poor in the east who had suffered most, Olivia knew. The fire was still a long way from the great houses of the western part of the city. It might even be brought under control before it reached them.

'Please God it will!' Olivia prayed in silence, thinking of the frightened townsfolk who had fled in that direction. Aloud, she said: "Henry — the children — do you think they'll still be safe? I must find them again —"

"They'll be safe," Benedict assured her with a tightening of the mouth. "I'm certain of that: their kind always survive."

"Perhaps," she conceded. "But it's going to be hard for them. They've lost almost everything."

"Don't let it trouble you. When all this is over I'll see they want for nothing — just so long as I have as little as possible to do with them afterwards."

His eyes moved to the dog cowering now near her feet. "Did you choose to come back for that creature, or were you ordered to?"

"Celia wanted someone to come, so I did," Olivia told him simply. She wanted to say: 'Why are we talking like this? What does it matter why I went back? All that matters is that we are here, together; and what that means for us both.'

Instead she said nothing more, and Benedict commented lightly: "Silly looking creature. I'd have left him to his fate."

It was almost as if he was trying to keep them both from talking of what must really occupy their minds, as if beneath the surface lay a minefield of painful emotions which he dared not, yet, bring into the light.

"Celia's very fond of him," Olivia said, taking her cue from him.

"She would be," said the Earl, in a tone which Celia would certainly not have appreciated.

There was a long silence, during which Olivia watched him as he gazed frowning at some prospect she could not see. And then he began abruptly: "Olivia, I . . ." and broke off almost at once. After a moment he tried again: "I found this waiting for me at Alston House, after I'd left you with your brother." He reached inside his doublet, and drew out a folded piece of paper, which he handed to her.

Puzzled, Olivia opened it. It was brief and unsigned, but she knew the writing at once.

Have a care, my lord, it said. *There are those who plot your death. I would not warn you, were it not for your wife. She loves you. You are not worthy of her, but if you live, cherish her as you would yourself.*

She read it twice through, her colour rising as she did so. She imagined Luke, struck suddenly by his conscience, pausing on his flight to send this warning note to the Earl — he was not to know it would have come too late. Or was it, rather, not conscience, but something else, stemming from his understanding of her, whom he loved, which had impelled him to write?

"I wonder how he knew," she murmured, scarcely realising she spoke aloud.

"Then it's true?" Benedict broke in. "That you —" Somehow he could not complete the sentence, but she knew what he meant to say, and gravely returned his gaze.

"Yes," she said quietly. "It's true. I think he must have known it before I did." She returned the note to him, and he refolded it carefully and put it away.

"I did not know what to think," he said, his voice hoarse now with the emotion he would not show. "It was Luke who wrote it, I suppose? I was angry when I read it — and then I began to wonder. Then, these past days I have been questioning the prisoners taken that night. From them I learned that you had indeed

187

taken no part in the plot — in fact, one told me that Luke had pressed you to help them, but you refused. So I knew that had not been why you came. I began, then, to hope a little — that was yesterday. I decided that today I would come and seek you, and tell you what I knew, and see if somehow things could be different between us. And then, at court, I heard talk of a fire, and knew it was close to you — and so I came —"

With a faint tremulous smile, Olivia reached out her hand and laid it in his.

"Thank God you did."

His fingers closed about hers, and he sat still, gazing into her eyes.

"Olivia, I wronged you — and myself, too, I think. Forgive me for that. But I fear that you may also unwittingly have wronged me. I learned from those prisoners that they believed me guilty of a most horrible conspiracy —"

Hope lit Olivia's face.

"Then it's not true? There was no plot? — But there must have been something —"

"It was not what you believed, I think. The negotiations came to nothing after all, so I am free to speak of them. We were indeed trying to win French support; but the price was not what you thought. We were ready, with the King's approval, to promise freedom of worship in England for believers of any religion, no matter what, so long as it did not threaten the peace of the realm. I think even your father would have approved of that."

Olivia considered for a moment, and then agreed.

"Yes, I think he would — but if only you had told me, right at the start!"

"I could not, then, be quite sure of you. After all, there are many of your persuasion who hate the idea of religious freedom if it means toleration for Catholics. For all I knew Luke was of that kind, and

188

I knew of your links with him — but, yes, I should have trusted you. I know now that you were always more loyal to me than I believed, even when —"

"Even when I did not know how much I loved you," she completed for him. "And I have cause to complain too that you did not tell me that you loved me."

He looked for a moment genuinely startled.

"I thought you could not fail to know that. Why else would I wish to marry you?"

"If you only knew the reasons I found for that! And not one of them the true one."

Gently, he drew her closer to him.

"You know now, don't you?" he whispered. She felt the hard lines of his body against hers, as she had feared never to do again, and his hands running caressingly down her back. She reached up and clasped her arms about him, and as his mouth came down on hers she whispered: "I know, my love, I know."

Later, much later, the boat drew smoothly into the shore where the gardens of Alston House reached the river. Benedict released her, and helped her in silence to her feet and onto the jetty, the dog in her arms; and then with his arm about her led her slowly along the path towards the house.

"You are welcome here as at Spensley, whatever I may once have said," he told her. "I shall not leave you there alone again. We shall go to court together. I do not want ever to be parted from you again as long as I live."

There was a pause while she returned his kiss, and then she said: "There may be someone else to keep me at Spensley when you go to court. In the spring, if all goes well —" And with great tenderness she told him what she meant, and watched the joy light his face as if in reflection of her own.